INHERITED DESTINY

Dan and Susan Huntington

Soul Attitude Press

Cover photo: Photo by Sasha Freemind on Unsplash

Published by Soul Attitude Press

Pinellas Park, FL

www.soulattitudepress.com

ISBN 978-1-946338-38-9 (print)

ISBN 978-1-946338-39-6 (Kindle)

Library of Congress Control Number: 2020908046

Printed in the United States of America

FIRST PRINTING

PROLOGUE

It was a bittersweet day in the Spring of 1941 when Catherine Simmons became an unwed mother at the tender age of eighteen. She gave birth to a beautiful baby girl. She named her Rachel after her paternal grandmother who had passed away just a year earlier. Despite the warnings from her parents about the consequences of poor choices, she had fallen for a charming, carefree, older college senior. Catherine experienced a hard lesson in human loyalty when the baby's father conveniently left the state upon hearing of her pregnancy.

She was fortunate to have wonderful, caring parents. Jim and Geraldine Simmons opened their home and welcomed the addition of baby Rachel. They did everything possible to provide a comfortable home for their daughter and granddaughter. Geraldine provided care during the day, enabling Catherine to work.

Catherine took a cashier job at a five and dime called W.T. Grant during the day. Her evenings were spent taking classes at Cuyahoga Community College, studying to be a nurse's aide. She cherished the few hours a day she could spend with her daughter. She was determined to provide a stable, happy environment despite her circumstances. Still suffering the emotional pain from the desertion of the baby's father, Catherine avoided the social scene, preferring to spend every available moment with little Rachel. Her routine was set and she was determined to graduate as soon as possible so she and her daughter could have a home of their own.

However, one Friday evening after class, some friends were able to coax her into meeting them for a drink at a local lounge called The Dew Drop Inn. After the long hours spent studying the last two years, Catherine looked forward to this short break from her usual routine. Knowing that her parents and Rachel were sleeping, Catherine didn't call home since she had planned on just staying a short time with her friends.

Early Saturday morning Geraldine heard her bedroom door open. She sat up to see her little two-year old granddaughter standing in the doorway hugging her stuffed Pooh Bear. In her soft sad voice, she said, "Grammy, where's mommy?"

Catherine's disappearance baffled the local police. They interviewed all her friends from school, including those who were with her the evening of her disappearance. They remembered that after having only one Margarita, she insisted on leaving. They described her walking out the door with the parting words, I gotta say good night to Rachel and Pooh Bear even though they're already sleeping. They recalled seeing her walk past the front window on her way to her car, smiling and giving one final wave.

The next day, police found her locked car in the parking lot. The only fingerprints on the vehicle were hers. She obviously never reached her car. No other clues. The detectives on the case tracked down Rachel's biological father who now lived in Minneapolis. He had not left that state in over a year. His alibi checked out. There were very little or no clues. The detectives, after exhausting what few leads they had, concluded that she had been abducted from the dark parking lot. Eventually her case went cold from lack of evidence and ended up in the dead case file.

Over time, Geraldine and James Simmons not only lost all hope of ever seeing their daughter again, but agonized that Rachel would never know her mother. Her biological father, after several attempts at communication, let them know that he wanted no part of being Rachel's father. He had moved on with his life. He was now married and his wife was expecting their first baby.

Geraldine and James Simmons adopted Rachel and raised her as their own daughter. Grammy and Papa were now the only family Rachel had left.

Over the next several years Rachel grew to be a bright young lady, very popular with her classmates and teachers. She had a winning personality, along with a keen sense of humor. Grammy and Papa beamed with pride, watching their Rachel walking in her poised manner to the podium. She gave an impressive valedictorian speech at her high school graduation.

College was her next goal. Rachel enrolled in Bradford University School of Veterinary Science. She graduated at the top of her class. Her grandparents again watched through joyful tears as she received her diploma and the distinction of summa cum laude.

After attending a couple celebration parties and enjoying countless hugs and handshakes, Rachel and her grandparents headed home to the little town of Northfield, Ohio. During the ninety-minute drive, Papa put the frosting on the cake. He announced that his friend Dr. Bill Reese, owner of Reese Animal Hospital, would like her to apply for an internship.

"Papa, you're kidding", Rachel screamed with delight from the backseat. "Oh my god, Papa, tell me you're not kidding me. This is incredible!"

Papa, smiling, glanced back for a second, drifting left and collided head-on with a semi-tractor trailer. Her grandparents were pronounced dead at the scene. Rachel was rushed to a nearby hospital in critical condition. She survived the night, but the doctors felt her injuries might be too severe and feared she could be left with permanent brain damage.

Rachel, being the sole remaining member of the Simmons family, had no one left to care for her. Still stunningly beautiful, yet with little hope of total recovery, she became a ward of the State of Ohio. Having no financial means of support, as soon as her physical wounds healed, she was moved to Pittsfield State Psychiatric Hospital, which became her permanent home.

Rachel's days at Pittsfield settled into one continuous pattern, day after day. A resident in cottage number three, she spent most days just gazing out the window at the beautiful oak trees and the grassy courtyard surrounded by additional patient cottages.

CHAPTER ONE

The Administrator at Pittsfield State Psychiatric Hospital, Dr. Herbert Graves, was a no-nonsense task master. Most of the attendants and staff referred to him as **Graveyard Graves** due to his dour personality. Intellectually, he was considered by the well-heeled, elite community of Shaker Heights to be the best of the best. "There are not many Rhodes scholars around," they would say. Some of the young psychologists, however, used another phrase in describing him. "God complex."

The staff was always prepared to look busy when he was around, and would then make a quick phone call to the next cottage warning them that Graveyard was coming their way. Always impeccably dressed, Dr. Graves walked with a slow, deliberate gait, his head high, but with his eyes looking downward, signaling he was not to be disturbed by idle chatter. The staff was accustomed to his glum expressions.

He had a penchant for calling staff meetings, which were usually a Dr. Graves' PowerPoint lecture given in a superior manner. These lectures would put a Chihuahua to sleep. Often, employees would get verbally dressed down if he decided to stop and ask a question and they didn't have a sufficient response. He periodically looked at his wristwatch, causing some to wonder, is he checking on the time or showing off his gold Rolex? He carried one of his many expensive Meerschaum pipes, though he didn't smoke. It was either a prop or an adult pacifier.

Second in command at Pittsfield, thirty-four-year-old Anna Frances, held the title of Deputy Administrator and was the polar opposite of Dr. Graves. Extremely energetic, running at least four marathons each year, she was known as the encourager by her peers. Her favorite saying was, "always try catching people in the act of doing something right;" a stark contrast to her boss. She was given a commendation by the Governor of Ohio for her exemplary contributions to mental health. Thus, Dr. Graves treated her with utmost respect. She made Graves look good to the brass in Columbus.

While on her daily rounds, Anna turned a

corner and nearly collided with Lisa Hunt, a young psychiatric aide working out of cottage number three. "Whoa!" she exclaimed as she grabbed Lisa to regain her balance.

"Lisa how are you and that beautiful baby doing?"

"We're doing fine ma'am, Lisa answered, "My husband Chris is spoiling her rotten."

"Lisa," Anna said with feigned authority, "what's this ma'am stuff! We're a team here so please call me Anna."

Lisa, with a slightly embarrassed grin, replied, "Thank you, Anna."

"Oh, and by the way, Lisa, I want you to know how much I appreciate the excellent job you're doing."

"I really try to do my best, that means a lot to me."

"So, Lisa, anything new going on in cottage three?"

"Well ma'am, um... Anna, we just admitted that new patient, Rachel Simmons."

"Yes, her story is very tragic."

"She's unbelievably beautiful. I felt so sad when I noticed her chart says the diagnosis is maybe irreversible brain damage."

"Yes, some things we just have no control

over. We'll just have to make her as comfortable as possible and hope for the best."

CHAPTER TWO

Over the next months, Rachel showed no improvement. She ate, drank and slept. Nothing else. The attendants tried everything imaginable to get a physical response. Everything from cartoons on TV to various kinds of music. Some of the aides would hold up pictures of puppies, kittens, and children, but nothing seemed to break through her catatonic state. Never a facial expression of joy, sadness, or fear.

One morning as Lisa Hunt was walking past Rachel's room, she heard a sound like someone choking. She hurried in to find Rachel lying on her back, throwing up, seemingly drowning in her own vomit. Lisa rolled her over, grabbed a small basin and a towel from the side table. After getting her partially cleaned up, she ran into the hall and yelled for help. The floor nurse appeared. After a quick examination, she told

Lisa it was most likely tainted food. Since that appeared to be a logical diagnosis, Lisa wasn't overly concerned. However, she became concerned when it happened the next day and the day after that.

Subsequently, her diet was closely monitored. It revealed she was given the same food as the other patients. Additional tests showed no infection. With the exception of a slightly elevated temperature, she appeared to be physically sound.

Staff Doctor Adams instructed the staff to monitor her for anything unusual and to report any changes.

Nurse Doria Goodwin, worked the night shift from 11 PM until 7 AM, and at the age of sixty-three would not consider retirement, as she loved her job. Since the passing of her husband six years ago, she found the job gave her some sense of purpose. The second shift had only one person on duty as the patients were, for the most part, sleeping. With little to do, Doria spent a good deal of her time reading patient's charts. One particular evening, Doria made a startling discovery as she read the file of Rachel Simmons. When Doria's shift ended, she stayed behind and requested a meeting with Dr. Adams.

Dr. Adams motioned her in as he carried a straight-backed chair to the corner of his small cubicle, placing it across from him. "Have a seat Doria," he said. "Would you care for some coffee or some water?"

"No, thank you, Dr. Adams," she said. "I noticed something last night and felt compelled to speak to you about it."

"Certainly, what is that Doria?" he said, leaning back in his chair, running his fingers through his salt and pepper hair.

"Well, doctor, while reading Rachel Simmons' chart last night," she paused briefly.

"Go on," said Dr. Adams leaning forward in his usual manner, fingers steepled, giving her his undivided attention.

"This may sound bizarre to you; but if I was a betting person, I'd bet that Miss Simmons is pregnant."

"Pregnant!" the doctor echoed back. "Doria, this is an all-female location," he exclaimed. "At night, medical support staff, even the cleaning people, are females. With the constant activity during the day shift, it would be virtually impossible. *Bizarre* might be an understatement indeed! What would lead you to this conclusion?"

"First off, Rachel appears to be suffering from morning sickness; but there's something more significant."

"What might that be?" Dr. Adams asked with a bit of condescension in his voice.

Alerted by his tone, Doria leaned back and crossed her arms in a defensive manner. "Well, doctor, while reading her chart last night, I noticed since the beginning her menstrual cycle was very regular and normal." She paused then and added, "except for the last two months."

"What? Are you telling me she's missed two periods?" the doctor asked, not so self-assured.

"Yes, that is what I'm saying."

Dr. Adams was silent as he leaned forward, appearing to be very troubled. Massaging his temple as if he had a migraine, he stood, indicating the meeting was over. "Thank you, Doria, for bringing this to my attention. As impossible as this seems, we'll take all proper measures in checking for a pregnancy."

Standing up, preparing to leave, she added, "Thank you for your time, doctor. I hope this has been helpful."

The next day Doria's suspicions were confirmed. Rachel Simmons was indeed found to be pregnant.

* * *

Seven months later, at 6:03 in the morning, Rachel Simmons was in the birthing room at Mercy Hospital in the process of delivering her baby. A feisty little boy came into the world kicking, screaming, clenching his tiny fist and waving his arms, resembling an adult trying to catch his balance while falling backwards.

The nurses hurriedly bathed him, suctioned his mouth and nostrils, and wrapped him in a warm blanket. An ordinary birth, no complications, all fingers and toes accounted for. Everyone in attendance agreed that he had an excellent set of lungs. Sadly, he would never see his mother, nor would she see him or hold him or hear him cry ever again.

Just as the team thought their job was about complete, they heard the doctor say, "Hold on there. Surprise! Surprise! it looks like we have another one!"

"What? Twins?" exclaimed the lead nurse, clearly shocked.

"Yep, it looks like we're getting two for the price of one," said the doctor, smiling.

The second baby was nothing like his twin brother. He was small, weak, and exhibited difficulty breathing. Baby number two was immediately transferred to the neo-natal intensive care unit at Mercy Hospital, while baby number one was transferred to an orphanage called Kinder-Kare, a state-run facility specializing in infants and toddlers. Like their mother, both babies became a ward of the State of Ohio.

With no next of kin to name the new born twins, the head nurse, having found the names of Rachel's grandparents, Geraldine and James Simmons, issued the birth certificate showing their names, Gerald and James.

Little James, or as the nurses called him, Jimmy, showed minimal progress while thirty miles away at Kinder-Kare Orphanage, Gerald continued to develop and was in excellent health. When couples came looking to adopt a child, Gerald was always among the first to capture their attention. The adoption was complicated by the fact that he was a twin and this agency, as others, had a policy against separating twins. However, after several weeks, Jimmy showed little or no improvement, prompting Kinder-Kare to make an exception. Gerald Simmons was cleared for adoption.

Within a month, one might say, "Baby Gerald hit the jackpot." A wealthy couple, Chad and

Becky Rawlins, were beyond ecstatic as they signed the papers and left with the son they had prayed for over the last five years. Owners of four automobile dealerships, European vacations, more money than they would ever need along with their huge house in Colorado Springs, meant nothing compared with the *gift* they received this day.

On the flight home, Becky could not stop whispering baby talk to her son. She could not stop calling him by his new name.

"Gerald Rawlins, you are so beautiful. Gerald, mommy loves you so much. Gerald this is daddy. Daddy, say something to Gerald."

"Hi Jerry," Chad said, pulling the blanket away from the baby's face.

"Jerry!" Becky said laughing, "his name is Gerald, Gerald Rawlins."

"Jerry sounds more like a car salesman," Chad teased.

"He's not going to be a car salesman; he's going to be a famous doctor. Aren't you Gerald?" she said, unable to take her eyes off her son.

"Mommy didn't have a problem with a car salesman when she met daddy," Chad said in a stage whisper to his son. This brought a laugh from Becky along with a loving punch in the arm. This went on for the entire trip while little Gerald slept through it all.

As the plane taxied to the gate, Becky looked at Chad and said through joyful tears, "Gerald or Jerry, car salesman or doctor, our prayers have been answered. We have a son."

CHAPTER THREE

Back in Ohio, Jimmy Simmons was eventually well enough to be discharged from the hospital and transferred to his new home, Kinder-Kare, where he would hopefully be adopted into a loving family, like his brother Gerald.

June 3rd, Jimmy's first birthday, was a day like any other day, no birthday cake or happy birthday song. No presents. No party. Just another entry in his seemingly endless charts. His chart read: "The child rarely cries or smiles. He has a passive reaction toward others and a preference to play alone."

When couples visited Kinder-Kare, they were invariably drawn to this beautiful blond-haired toddler with the deep-set green eyes, until they heard of his birth mother being a patient in a mental institution. Imagining the father may possibly be a psychopath or God knows what, they turned their attention elsewhere. The staff at Kinder-Kare came to accept the reality that Jimmy, though adorable, could be unadoptable. With each passing year, his chances of adoption diminished. Their only viable option became a suitable foster home.

* * *

At the age of seven, Jimmy entered his first of many foster homes. Phil and Martha Carrington had three children of their own; but they found housing foster children cheaper than hiring farmhands for their produce farm. The day seven-year-old Jimmy, along with his social worker, arrived at the Carrington's farm, he appeared in awe of the foreign surroundings. He moved his head side to side, attempting to absorb everything at once. He'd never seen so many trees and open fields. It was all new and confusing. Although he showed little emotion when meeting Phil and Martha, Jimmy was somewhat apprehensive when he met David and Freddy, the Carrington's two older boys who were a few years older and much bigger.

Mr. and Mrs. Carrington showed him his room that he would share with their youngest son, Alex, who was only five years old. It had two twin beds, both showing colorful quilts covered in animal pictures. Before turning off the light, Mrs. Carrington said, "We're glad to have you with us, Jimmy. I hope you will be happy here. Get a good night's sleep, tomorrow we are going to have fun pulling weeds in the strawberry field."

When Mrs. Carrington closed the door, he looked over at Alex, who was curled up hugging his pillow apparently fast asleep. Jimmy pulled his covers up to his chin, stared at the ceiling, and laid there wondering what tomorrow might bring.

He woke up to the aroma of bacon and a cacophony of chatter coming from another room. He looked over at the other bed and noticed Alex was already up. Getting dressed, he followed the sound coming from the kitchen.

"Well, good morning Jimmy," greeted Mrs. Carrington. "Did you sleep well last night?"

He nodded, not having anything to say.

"Why are you wearing shoes?" Freddy chirped in, 'we don't wear shoes in the summertime."

"Jimmy you can wear your shoes or go barefoot; it's up to you," Mr. Carrington said while patting him on the shoulder as he walked to the table.

He stiffened at the touch. He looked at Alex and mumbled, "I'll go barefoot like Alex."

Jimmy thought the bacon, scrambled eggs and potatoes was the best meal he ever had. He was quick to clean his plate and drain his tall glass of milk. He watched Alex take his plate to the sink, so he walked around the table to do the same. Except for a few words, he remained quiet since entering the kitchen. He hoped maybe this was going to be a good place.

"Let's go guys, the weeds are growing and we gotta get a jump on it," Mr. Carrington announced. "David, you show Jimmy how to pull the weeds and be careful not to harm the strawberry plants."

Jimmy caught on quickly, pulling weeds without complaint, stopping only to eat a few strawberries, like the other boys. He enjoyed the country air, the feel of dirt between his toes and the smell and taste of ripe strawberries.

Mr. and Mrs. Carrington were friendly enough and Jimmy was relieved that they didn't get too close. This suited him just fine; he didn't like being touched.

He soon learned that David and Freddie, the two older boys, had a penchant for teasing, so he was careful to give them a wide berth.

He was content to pull weeds and be left alone. The only apparent chink in his emotional armor was a German Shepherd named Buck. The dog would sidle up to him in the field and lick his face. He soon became attached to the dog and somehow Buck had sensed the boy's inner pain and suffering. Often in the evening when the chores were done, the Carrington's would find him outside in the darkest corner of the yard sitting alone with Buck. Jimmy fanaticized what it would be like to have a real family and dog like Buck. He sat petting the dog until his dreams were interrupted by Mrs. Carrington's call, "Bedtime."

Like most younger brothers, Alex was a constant target for taunts and pranks from David and Freddie. Alex now had an ally in Jimmy who shared the good-natured harassment until, unfortunately, it got out of control.

One evening, Dave and Freddie crept up behind Jimmy and dropped a harmless, but very large, rat snake around his neck. He screamed as he tried batting the snake away, but the snake seemed to be everywhere at the same time. He rolled over and over in the grass screaming and flailing his arms. He felt absolute terror.

When he escaped and the snake slithered away, Jimmy ran blindly into the night. Tears streaming, briars and branches slapping his face, he came to a road. He crossed the road into a cornfield on the opposite side when he stumbled and fell into a barbed wire fence, cutting his arms, legs and face. He pushed to his feet and ran deep into the corn. Exhausted, he fell to the ground, his lungs burning, as he gasped for air; his face stinging from the tears running into his wounds. He sat motionless, hugging his knees. As his breathing slowed, he became aware of the absolute quiet, the stillness of the night. A sense of peace stole over him as he realized he was safe.

The silence was shattered by the sound of screeching tires coming from the road, followed by a dull thud and an agonizing howl.

In the early morning hours, the family found him sitting in a ditch cradling Buck in his lap. Jimmy was rocking back and forth, staring in a catatonic state. He was taken by ambulance to a local hospital and treated for shock and minor abrasions. The next day he was returned to Kinder-Kare. Several weeks passed before he appeared to have recovered from his traumatic experience at the farm.

After a few more unsuccessful attempts at various foster homes, the agency feared they might never find a suitable foster home for this poor, unfortunate child.

CHAPTER FOUR

While reading through a stack of applications, the Director saw one prospective foster couple that just might be a fit. John and Sarah Barnes were in their early forties, devout Christians, who volunteered at a local homeless shelter. They were active in the First Baptist Church of Salem, a small, northeastern Ohio town. They were financially secure due to a generous inheritance from John's deceased parents. The Director thought this was a great option being the boy required close attention and extensive care. After a thorough background check, John and Sarah Barnes were approved.

On the appointed day, they arrived at precisely 8:30 AM. The secretary welcomed them and could not help but notice their plain, old-fashioned appearance. Sarah's hair was braided and rolled into a tight bun. She wore no makeup and her plain cotton flowered dress was reminiscent of the flour-sack dresses seen on the popular television series, Little House on the Prairie. She smelled of ivory soap and when she smiled her entire gums showed. She could not stop smiling in anticipation of meeting their first, hopefully only, foster child. Adoption was her dream.

John wore green work pants and a short-sleeved plaid shirt complete with a pocket protector advertising Wonder Bread. The secretary observed his baby-faced, ruddy complexion, thinking he resembled Elmer Fudd with his perfectly combed and sprayed hair. A style people referred to as TV evangelist hair. Her eyebrows lifted when she saw him tightly clutching a King James Bible in his right hand.

The matronly caseworker walked into the room as Sarah gushed, "Praise the Lord, I'm so excited. God has provided, just like you said he would, John."

"Matthew 19:14," John replied.

"Pardon me?" inquired the caseworker, a bit taken back at John's remark.

"*Suffer the little children and forbid them not to come unto me: for of such is the kingdom of heaven*, Matthew 19:14," John said in a pious manner, hands folded and eyes staring upward.

"Whatever," said the caseworker, clearly confused by John's recitation. "I'll go get Jimmy."

A few minutes later she walked back into the room with one arm around the boy's shoulder carrying a black plastic bag containing his meager belongings.

"Mr. and Mrs. Barnes, this is Jimmy," she announced.

"James, not Jimmy," interrupted John.

"Excuse me?" she said. "I don't understand."

"His name is James," John repeated. "James, was the elder son of Zebedee, brother of John, my namesake, one of the twelve apostles. Sarah, James, let's be going. It's Wednesday, we have prayer meeting this evening and much to do tomorrow. Another thing, young man, you are to address us as Mr. John and Miss Sarah. Is that understood?"

Jimmy nodded, staring at his feet, tensing up at Mr. John's stern attitude.

"Well, whatever," the caseworker mumbled to herself. Before turning over the documents, she gently squeezed Jimmy's shoulder in an effort to reassure him.

"Here are your copies of the documents you both signed. You have our number and the number of James' social worker. Please don't hesitate to call if you need anything, anything at all."

The caseworker followed them out and watched as the three drove away in a green pickup truck belching smoke. On the tailgate a bumper sticker read, *God is my copilot.*

* * *

Sarah taught children's Sunday school and looked forward to taking her new foster son to church. She was the proverbial mother hen, reading Bible stories to Jimmy until he dozed off at night. She would sing to him incessantly during the day, "Jesus loves the little children, all the children of the world, be they yellow, black or white; they are precious in his sight. Jesus loves the little children of the world." Jimmy didn't speak much but appeared to enjoy the songs. Sarah, with God's help, was determined to bring this lost lamb out of the wilderness into the heavenly flocks.

John, however, was the polar opposite of his wife. Jimmy couldn't remember ever seeing him smile, or for that matter, have much to say. When John did speak, his comments usually included a verse from the Bible. If he failed to follow a request from Miss Sarah, John would say, "James, children must obey their parents; Ephesians 6:1. Do you want God to punish you? Do you understand?"

"Yes," Jimmy mumbled.

"Yes what?"

"Yes, I understand, I don't want God to punish me, Mr. John."

One morning when he failed to come to breakfast, Sarah went into his room and found him hiding under his bed. She coaxed him out and led him into the kitchen. Sarah noticed he was more withdrawn this day than usual. She attempted to cheer him up by reciting one of her Sunday school nursery rhymes, but Jimmy's eyes remained fixed on his oatmeal. When John entered the kitchen, he jumped out of his chair and bolted from the room, screaming in hysterics as he ran from the house. Sarah finally caught him before he reached the busy Route 30, which ran past their property. It was all she could do to wrestle him back to the house while he was kicking and screaming, "No, no."

When they got back inside, John was gone. Jimmy sat facing the corner rocking back and forth with his eyes closed and his fist so tightly clenched that his fingernails nearly drew blood from his palms.

Sarah sat beside him softly singing, Jesus loves me.

Then, when John walked back into the room, the hysterics began all over again. Sarah prayed for Jimmy to be delivered from what her husband referred to as *Satan's grip.*

"Second Corinthians 2:11" he quoted, "*Lest Satan should get an advantage of us for we are not ignorant of his devices.*"

This scene continued for several days with Sarah trying everything she could to reach him. She tried to question him, but he remained silent and would only start crying when she pushed too hard. Out of despair, Sarah called the social worker.

After listening to Sarah's explanation of the events, the social worker became very alarmed. She documented all the details that Sarah had provided and informed her they would be there as soon as possible to remove him from their home. When she hung up the phone, she made arrangements for Jimmy to be returned to the orphanage immediately.

Sarah was required to file out an exit report which filled several pages. In her report, one comment caught the attention of the staff. Sarah stated that at first Jimmy was quiet, but respectful to John. But one day, every-thing changed and just the sight of John would send him into hysterics. Sarah stated that she thought perhaps John's stern discipline could be the cause.

Jimmy was back home at Kinder-Kare, se-cure in his safe haven with the shiny Terrazzo floors, green walls and the familiar smell of urine and pine sol. Everything seemed back to normal, except when the attendants had to sedate him in the middle of the night. He would wake up screaming and crying as if having a nightmare. If only he could tell somebody about the terror of John's midnight visit. Of waking up feeling John's hands on his shoulders, hold-ing him down, and the terrible pain. The awful smell of his putrid breath as he whispered in his ear, "If you tell anybody, God will punish you." Jimmy didn't understand what happened; but he knew it was bad, very bad, and it hurt. But he was home now and the social worker promised him he would never have to see Mr. John again.

Child psychologist, Dr. Joyce Kerbeck, was called in to interview the youngster.

"Jimmy, is there anything you would like to tell me about Mr. John?"

"Mr. John is a bad man," he blurted in an angry tone.

"Why is Mr. John a bad man?" she asked.

With that he totally shut down, with tears welling up in his eyes. He would not respond to further questions. Too much time had passed for a physical examination to prove anything, but the staff had their suspicions. With no evidence, all they could do was permanently remove the Barnes from any further consideration as foster parents. They hoped in time, Jimmy would overcome the trauma that he suffered, whatever it was.

Four long years passed with Jimmy being moved to several more foster homes, none of which worked out well for one reason or another. The State of Ohio was buying time until a better option became available.

CHAPTER FIVE

The following year, with great fanfare, the Governor of Ohio stood before a cheering crowd and cut the ribbon, officially opening Shady Hills Psychiatric Hospital for Emotionally Disturbed Children. The purpose of this facility was to treat only emotionally disturbed children, ages six to sixteen. They did not admit children with chromosomal issues, only those who the doctors believed could re-enter society within two years.

Shady Hills was located on twelve acres of land in a rural area approximately seven miles from the nearest town. It was a single-story structure, except for a gymnasium that doubled as a theater for movies, guest speakers and other public events. The layout was a series of rooms called pods, each with six bedrooms containing a set of twin beds. The pods were divided according to age. Half the pod was carpeted with couches and easy chairs where the children could watch television. The other half of the room had tile floors and a large table where the children could eat family-style. All the children were given chores, like cleaning up after dinner, mopping the floor, and general housekeeping. Each child was expected to make their own bed and keep their room in good order, thus being compatible with the average American household.

Unlike the typical state hospital, Shady Hills was designed to have comfortable, homey surroundings. The floors were carpeted, pictures adorned the walls, colors were bright and cheery, creating a pleasing environment. There were no bars on the windows. Shady Hills policy regarding staff attire was also different. Doctors, R.N.'s and attendants wore casual clothing, thereby promoting a nonthreatening atmosphere. The doctors advisory committee set the Hospital's standards. The programs strived to provide as normal an environment for the children as possible. Children were treated in the least restrictive way, thereby encouraging them to be self-sufficient. Children would have access to educational, psychological, and social services appropriate to their needs. Activities would be all-inclusive, affording each child a sense of self-worth.

Anna Frances couldn't contain her excitement when she learned she was being transferred from Pittsfield State Mental Hospital and promoted to the position of Director at Shady Hills. Touring the facility for the first time, Anna was impressed with her surroundings and was anxious to get started on this new challenge. The only down side was that she still was under the authority of Dr. Graves, who was now the Director over all the facilities in the region.

Assembling her staff, Anna began interviewing candidates to fill the position of Assistant Director. After her most recent interview was complete, she began thumbing through her papers in search of the final application to be considered that day. She hoped this last applicant would prove to be the one. Although the previous applicants were qualified, they didn't have that special desire to make a difference in the children's lives. This last applicant was a Mr. Dale Karsten, home town, Luthersburg, Pennsylvania, age twenty-three. He was due to arrive in fifteen minutes. Turning slightly, she saw movement outside her window. Anna watched as a white VW Beetle with a Pennsylvania license plate pulled into the parking space. She assumed it was probably him. She observed him looking into his rearview mirror as he ran a comb through his hair. She found it amusing watching him extract himself from the small car. She noticed he stood at least six foot three as he grabbed his suit coat from the back seat and put it on. He looked at his reflection in the car window, adjusted his tie before proceeding into the building. She observed he walked with a long confident stride.

A few minutes later, she heard a tap on her open door. Looking up and motioning him in, she was immediately impressed by Dale's warm and friendly personality. He walked toward her, extended his hand, and with relaxed confidence, introduced himself.

"Miss Frances?" Dale asked with a smile.

"Please, have a seat Dale. . . I'm not big on formalities, so please call me Anna."

"Thank you, Anna, I appreciate this opportunity to meet with you today."

"So, what brings you from Pennsylvania to this neck of the woods?"

"I read about Shady Hills and its unique concept. It felt like a perfect fit for me."

"Before we discuss the position, tell me a little about you, the person."

"Well, I was born the only son of Harold and Mary Karsten. I apparently inherited my Nordic features and size from my father. We own and live on a dairy farm in Western Pennsylvania, where I learned the value of hard work. In high school I was a jock, playing all the sports. Though I got excellent grades, I didn't particularly enjoy school."

After high school, I enrolled at Penn State University. I stayed there until I completed my Associate's Degree in Psychology. I enjoyed my Psychology courses but had enough of book learning. I was anxious to get involved in some type of practical application."

"When I read about this new hospital, I sent my resume, packed up my belongings and headed for the Buckeye State. My parents supported my decision and pointed out to me what my grandfather often said, *"There's a big difference between book smarts and wisdom."*

"So, here I am!"

Anna responded with a smile, making a spontaneous decision. "You have an interesting background and excellent credentials for the job. I feel your outgoing personality will take you far with the children. So, let's take some time going over the details and if you agree, I can set you up for the psychiatric aide class starting next Monday. As my Assistant, this is the first class you will need to complete. It's a two-day class covering the aspects of your job along with hospital protocol."

Dale replied, "I'm excited to accept this position. I'm currently staying at the Motel 6. I'll take the next few days locating an apartment and getting settled in."

"There's some nice-looking apartments on Sagamore Road you might want to check out. I heard their prices are reasonable. They advertise a club house along with a pool and tennis courts."

"That sounds nearly perfect. I'll look into them first thing tomorrow."

"It's all settled then, I'll see you on Monday. In the meantime, if you need anything further, you can contact me here at the hospital."

Dale stood, shook her hand and left.

Anna felt confident in her selection and as Dale opened the car door, she found it even more humorous seeing him squeezing his tall frame into that little VW.

* * *

The next morning, Dale visited the apartment complex which Anna had suggested. He found it to be an excellent place, very suitable for his needs. The next item on his to-do list was to open up a bank account.

Dale entered the First Bank of Bedford Heights and waited until the new accounts manager was available. Her name plate read Susan Collins. Dale found her to be extremely attractive. He always felt drawn to tall, thin brunettes. The first thing he did was check her left hand and was pleased to see no ring. He noticed her big brown eyes and genuine wide smile revealing perfect teeth, which added to her beauty.

After organizing the papers on her desk, she looked up and asked, "What can we do for you today?"

Dale opened the conversation. "I just moved here from Pennsylvania and accepted a position at the new Shady Hills Hospital. For starters, I'm going to need a checking account. I have a savings account at my bank back home, but I'll wait to transfer that later."

"All right then, let's get started," she said while removing a form from her file. "Okay, full name?"

"Dale Andrew Karsten. When my mother used all three, I knew I was in trouble," Dale joked.

"Complete mailing address and phone number?"

"Sagamore Hills Apartments, 681 Sagamore Rd., Apt. 37. My phone is being installed today. I'll call you when I get my new number."

"Okay, if married, I'll need your spouse's name."

"Single, still looking for the right girl." At that Dale detected a very slight but unmistakable smile as she looked up from her papers and made eye contact. This caused his hopes to soar.

Gaining a little confidence, Dale proceeded with caution. "Being new in town, I haven't the slightest idea where I am half the time. I could certainly use a local friend. Perhaps you could help me to find my way around," he said, with a mock helpless look in his eyes.

Susan pushed the file aside, leaned forward and gave Dale the most beautiful smile he had ever seen. "I've only lived here a few months myself and don't know what kind of tour guide I'd make. This may be a little unprofessional, but my instincts tell me I should help a friend in need. The First Bank of Bedford Heights is known for its helpful customer service, so how can I be of assistance?" she said, playing along with his flirtatious personality.

"Well," Dale replied, "perhaps you could recommend an excellent restaurant where two people could enjoy a quiet dinner."

Putting her hand on the telephone as though preparing to make a call, she said, "What are the names of the two people? I'd be happy to make reservations for you," she said, trying to keep a straight face.

"Well," Dale said, "that would be Mr. Dale Karsten, and the other one would be . . . " He paused for a second, and said, "What is your last name again?" With that they both laughed loud enough to get the attention of some other customers in the bank. Putting her finger to her lips, she said in a whisper, "It's Susan, Susan Collins."

"Well Susan Collins, would you consider joining a poor lonely stranger for dinner this evening?"

With that, Susan scribbled a note and slowly slid it across the desk. Dale picked up the note and read it.

"Thank you," he said, "I'll be there. Jonny's

Steak & Seafood, 360 Chestnut Avenue at 7:00 PM. Perfect. I think I'm going to like this town." With that, Dale stood up, shook her hand in a professional manner and left the bank.

Dale arrived early and asked the Hostess for a table in a quiet corner. He no sooner sat down when he saw Susan approaching the table. Dale had been trying to come up with a clever opening line but it was too late, he'd just have to go with the flow. Dale stood up, circled the table and pulled her chair out. "You caught me day dreaming," Dale said while sitting back down.

"And what were you day dreaming about?" she asked with a teasing tone in her voice.

"I was trying to think of a clever remark that would impress you, to be honest."

"Well, that in itself impresses me. I'm flattered."

"As long as we're being candid, I have a small confession of my own."

"And what would that be?" Dale asked.

"Do you remember the question I asked you on your application about the name of your spouse?"

"Yes, yes I do."

"Well," she said with a sheepish grin, "there's

no such question on the form, but I was curious as to your marital status."

"You little rascal. Now it's my turn to be flattered."

The waiter approached their table, asking them what they would like to drink. Dale extended an open hand toward Susan, indicating ladies before gentlemen.

"I'd like a zinfandel please," she said, looking up at the waiter.

"And make mine a Cabernet, California if you have it," Dale said.

While they were waiting for their drinks, Dale visually surveyed the dining room and remarked to Susan, "This place certainly has a warm appealing atmosphere; you made an excellent choice."

"Some friends at the bank recommended this restaurant when I first moved here. I've been here a couple times and never had a bad experience."

When their drinks arrived, Dale lifted his glass and said, "So, Miss Collins, what shall we drink to?"

Susan slowly rubbed her chin, emulating one who is deep in thought. "How about we just say, cheers? How's that for being original?"

Dale smiled, raising his glass, "I'll drink to that. Cheers," as they clinked their glasses.

"What's this place famous for?" Dale asked while scanning the menu.

"It's the most popular steak restaurant in this area, but I love their oak grilled swordfish."

"Swordfish? Hmm," Dale said, swirling his glass and taking a sip of wine. "I must admit I've never had swordfish in my life. Growing up on a farm, our staples were meat and potatoes." Putting his glass down he added, "You might say I'm just a country boy."

"And I'm a city girl," she said, brushing her long dark hair from her eyes. "But you know what they say, opposites attract. You can have a taste of my fish and I guarantee you will be hooked, no pun intended."

While enjoying dinner, they each painted a picture of their lives growing up. Susan explained that her dad was a CPA who had encouraged her to get a degree in accounting. "So, you see, if it weren't for my dad, I wouldn't be working at the bank and we would've never met," she said with a chuckle. "My mom, on the other hand, is the perfect example of a great home maker. To my benefit, she chose not to work, so we are not only mother and daughter, but best friends. I was the envy of my class-mates, they always congregated at our house, all being spoiled by Mom's fresh bread and pas-tries. I wish I could still live at home, but it would be too long a drive from Ashland to the bank every day. Being an only child, I miss my parents terribly. I do go home for weekends as often as I can."

"Well, I've never met your mom or dad, but if I ever do, I'll thank your dad for encouraging you to major in accounting, resulting in our date tonight. And your mom sounds like a carbon copy of mine. We have something else in common. I'm an only child as well."

After dinner they ordered key lime pie and coffee. As the evening progressed, they found conversation came easy.

In the middle of their conversation, Dale looked around and said, "Susan, do you re-alize this place is practically empty!" He looked at his watch and said, "We've been here over three hours."

Susan replied with a wide smile, "You know what they say, time flies when you 're having a good time, and I've had a great time tonight."

Dale stood, pulled her chair back, "I had a wonderful time too, and I would love to do this again, real soon." He walked her to her car as Susan fished into her purse and handed him a card listing her home address and phone number. As she handed it to him, she said, "You might need this!"

Dale answered, "I don't have a card, but when I do, you'll be the first to get one. I'm looking forward to starting my new job on Monday. They will most likely supply me with business cards." Not really wanting to leave, he said, "I still have some loose ends to tie up this weekend, so I better be going."

"Well, thank you again for a wonderful evening, please let me know how you enjoyed your first day on your new job."

"I promise," Dale said as he gave her a quick hug and a peck on her cheek.

He stood in the parking lot watching her drive away, knowing in his heart that there really was such a thing as *love at first sight*.

Obviously, Susan felt the same, because over the next four months being virtually inseparable, they became engaged.

CHAPTER SIX

Dale took to his new job with enthusiasm. He was assigned to the ten to twelve-year old's which was in fact his favorite age group. His days were filled with new challenges. The staff at Shady Hills were impressed with his natural ability to communicate with the children. They all agreed he had the patience of Job.

A few weeks into his first month, a new patient, James Simmons, now eleven years old, was admitted to Shady Hills. He arrived on a Monday and was met by Dale Karsten.

"Jimmy, my name is Dale Karsten. I'm here to show you around and to help you get settled. We're happy to have you with us."

Dale picked up Jimmy's black plastic bag containing the child's worldly possessions. "Let's go," Dale said as he laid his right hand on his shoulder. Jimmy stiffened at the touch, so Dale removed his hand and stuffed it into his pocket.

With an understanding smile, he said, "Let's take a look around your new home. This is the gym. Through that door is a swimming pool. Do you like to swim?"

"Don't know how," Jimmy mumbled, looking at his shoes.

"Well, you'll learn if you want. If not, you don't have to," Dale said in a reassuring voice.

Still showing no reaction, Jimmy continued to follow Dale.

"Okay, down here are the rooms where you'll take classes five days a week. There are no first, second or third grades. You'll move up at your own pace in each subject. We have a very large playground outside. I think you're really gonna like it here, Jimmy."

Still no reaction.

"Let's go see your room," Dale said as they walked together down the long hallway. "This is your room. Your bed is here by the door."

As Dale pointed out the various features, Jimmy walked over to his bed, stood quietly and started lightly rubbing the navy-blue bedspread. He gently touched the shade of his bedside lamp. His expression, Dale noticed, was one of wonderment, as though he had never seen anything so nice.

The nearby family room erupted with a blare of children's voices and a scurry of activity. "All right guys, put your stuff in your rooms and get washed up for dinner," an attendant yelled over the chaos.

Jimmy turned to see a small black boy standing in the doorway with a book bag hanging over his shoulder. He eyed his new roommate with a suspicious look as he slid around him and dropped the bookbag on his bed.

"Jimmy, this is Troy Green. Troy, say hi to your roommate, Jimmy Simmons." Dale smiled down at the two youngsters who were still sizing each other up.

Troy broke the silence with a question. "What did you do?" he asked.

"Nuthin," he said chewing on his thumbnail.

"My mom put me in here because she can't handle me, why'd your mom put you in here?"

"Don't have one," he mumbled.

"Don't have what?" Troy demanded.

"A mom."

"The dude don't say much, does he?" Troy said squinting up at Dale.

Dale answered, "That's okay, Troy, you say enough for two people."

While playfully ruffling Troy's hair, he urged

them forward to the bathroom. "Come on guys, let's wash up for dinner."

Dale led the way into the family room where most of the kids ran up to him, all talking at the same time. He took time to exchange a few words with each boy before directing them to the tables for the homestyle meal that had been wheeled in on a stainless-steel food cart. Jimmy enjoyed the meatloaf and mashed potatoes, but sat staring at his plate, sliding the green beans back and forth until they were dismissed.

As days turned into weeks and weeks into months, Jimmy gradually adapted to his new surroundings. For the first time in his life, he felt a sense of belonging. School was less intimidating than the public schools he'd attended while living in foster homes. The swimming pool became his favorite place, though he was careful not to venture near the deep end.

Still preferring to be alone, he usually avoided the other children when at all possible. He did, however, look forward to the days Mr. Karsten would be on duty, and often found himself looking out at the parking lot for the familiar white V.W. beetle.

One morning as Dale pulled into his usual parking space, he saw Jimmy looking out the window. He couldn't tell for sure, but he would've bet next week's paycheck that the kid smiled. He was so sure he intended to make a note of it in his chart tonight. God knows that chart could use a few positives for a change.

As Assistant Director, Dale would occasionally work the night shift in order to become familiar with the complete scope of the job. One particular evening, after the boys had all gone to their rooms, Dale sat down in his small staff office reading the patient charts from the day shift. While making his own notations he felt someone's presence. Looking up from his work, he met the green eyes of Jimmy Simmons standing there watching him work.

"Well, hi there big guy!" Dale said laying his paperwork aside. "You having trouble sleeping? he asked with genuine concern.

"Yeah."

"Bad dreams?"

"No."

Dale stood up, walked around his desk and sat on one of the chairs in front of Jimmy. Now at eye level Dale gently placed his hands on his shoulders. "So, what's up, you wanna talk?"

Jimmy stood there saying nothing, fidgeting with the buttons on his pajama top. Dale sensed he had something on his mind, but didn't know how to express himself.

"Jimmy, is there anything you want to know? Any questions you'd like to ask me?"

A fleeting expression on his face told Dale that he was on the right track.

"You know," Dale began, "I know many things about your life. In fact, I know all the way back to the day you were born. You see, the people in hospitals, here at Shady Hills and even the foster families, kept notes on a chart like this." Dale held up the chart for him to see. "It's kinda like the story of your life."

"Is that one mine?" Jimmy asked.

"No," said Dale, laying the file aside again. "This is somebody else's, but yours looks just like it."

Dale noticed he didn't seem to resent there being a file about him, in fact, he appeared somewhat interested and maybe even a bit proud that someone would write a story about him.

"So, you see, there isn't much I don't know about you. You can ask me anything, anything at all."

Jimmy looked down, examining his fingernails for a moment, then slowly raised his eyes to Dale. "Do you have a mother and a father?"

"Yes, I do," said Dale, not knowing what to say next, completely caught off guard.

Silent emotion hung in the air like cigar smoke in a pool hall.

"Where are they?" Jimmy asked.

"They live on a dairy farm in Pennsylvania where I grew up."

"I saw a picture of a dairy farm once on the calendar," he said in a flat tone, while rocking from one foot to the other. "There were cows and a big red building."

Dale thought, *my god, to be institutionalized for your entire life, what must it be like? Never to go to a mall, or a drug store, or a movie theater. Things he took for granted all his life must be foreign to this little kid. The system diagnoses him as mentally disturbed, writes his daily history in their damnable charts. The shrinks hold their weekly interviews, and pigeonhole him into one of their favorite categories like psychotic, neurotic, or schizophrenic. At the end of the day, they hop in their Porsche or BMW and drive home with a warm fuzzy feeling like they performed some great humanitarian service, when, in fact, their system is what made Jimmy what he is today.*

Keeping his eyes on Jimmy, Dale pulled the

second chair closer to his desk, motioning him to sit down.

"That big red building was a barn."

Jimmy eyes widened, "Did you have horses too?"

"Yes, we rode horses a lot on the farm. As a kid, I used to pretend I was a cowboy."

"I've noticed you seem to like the pool, don't you?"

"Well, yeah, but not the deep end."

"Did you know you could breathe underwater?" Dale asked.

"Oh no," he chuckled, "I could never do that, I know I could never do that."

"It's called scuba diving. Do you know what scuba diving is?"

"No, I've never heard of that, either."

"Well, one day next week when I'm back on day shift, I'll bring my scuba gear so you and all your friends can breathe underwater in the pool."

Jimmy actually smiled at the thought. A real honest to goodness 500-watt smile.

"We'll do it next week, I promise, but you better hit the rack now, it's getting pretty late. Have a good night and I'll see you after school tomorrow."

Jimmy stood up, started out the door, then paused.

"What is it?"

"You'll be there, you won't let me drown?"

"I will not let you drown. I promise. You're really going to enjoy it."

Jimmy smiled again and disappeared into his room.

Dale wanted to scream, there is nothing wrong with that kid. He grabbed Jimmy's chart and filled three pages. He couldn't stop smiling.

* * *

Over the next few months, Dale spent a great deal of his off time working with Jimmy and a couple of the other boys. Not only did he learn to scuba, but with the confidence he gained, Jimmy soon learned to swim. During regular swim sessions Jimmy would dive with enthusiasm into the deep end and join the other kids in a pool game called Marco Polo. He was the first one in; the last one out. During gym class, Dale also taught him the best way to throw and catch a football, and play a respectable game of ping-pong.

Thanksgiving was coming up in a few weeks and the majority of the patients would be going home to their families for an extended weekend. In fact, Jimmy was the only boy from his pod not scheduled to leave the hospital. Thinking about this, Dale came up with a plan of his own.

He went to see Anna Frances to ask permission to sign him out for the holiday weekend. He had plans to have Thanksgiving at the home of his fiancés' parents, Mr. and Mrs. Collins. Dale had told them about the unfortunate child. They encouraged Dale to bring him along.

Anna was very understanding, but reluctant to take responsibility. After a long discussion, she denied the weekend leave, but relented to allow Dale to take him out for the day. 8 AM to 8 PM. Dale was satisfied with half a victory. He was determined to make it a day this kid would never forget.

At 7:30 AM Dale was at the front desk filling out and signing a volume of release forms required before removing a patient from the facility. Soon they were on their way in the little white VW beetle.

Their first stop was Raintree State Park, where they hiked a nature trail, walked across a ravine, over a suspension bridge that swung back and forth as they walked. Jimmy was apprehensive at first but with a little encouragement from Dale, was soon standing in the middle of the bridge spitting in the water below.

From there, they walked about half a mile to a petting zoo, where Jimmy fed goats, petted a calf, and saw a llama for the first time in his life. When they exited the petting zoo area, Dale spotted a small take-out café and realized it was lunch time. He ordered a hamburger for each of them and while eating, enjoyed the relaxed chatter from Jimmy, that was so much out of character.

"Jimmy, would you like a hot fudge sundae or a banana split?"

He answered, "I don't know, I've never had either one."

Dale thought it over and said, "We'll get one of each and we can share."

When they finished, Dale asked, "So which one did you like best?"

Jimmy grinned, "I don't know. I loved them both!"

They walked back to the parking lot and were soon off to the Collins' for Thanksgiving dinner.

They approached the large brick ranch style house which set back into a grove of fir trees. As they got out of the car, Jimmy found himself ankle-deep in autumn leaves. He reached down and picked up a double handful and threw them into the air. Dale watched as it rained brown and gold. The look in his eyes confirmed to Dale that he'd chosen the perfect vocation. Dale was aware Susan and her parents were waiting for them inside, but he was not going to hurry Jimmy's adventure. This was his day.

Entering the house, Jimmy was hit with multiple sensations at the same time. The heat in the house, in contrast to the crisp November breeze outside, made him a little dizzy. His stomach growled as he smelled the combination of turkey, oyster dressing, and pumpkin pie.

The living room smelled of firewood and furniture polish. On the far wall was a fireplace, aglow and crackling, surrounded by a sectional sofa. In front of a large picture window stood a baby grand piano. Jimmy noticed a squirrel playing outside the window. It reminded him of a picture he once saw in one of his foster homes.

"We're here," Dale yelled loud enough to be heard over the chatter coming from the kitchen. Three people appeared at the same time, all wearing aprons, even the gray-haired old guy.

Dale rested his arm lightly on his shoulder and said, "This is my friend, Jimmy Simmons."

"Jimmy, this is Mr. and Mrs. Collins and their daughter, Susan."

"We're so glad you could come Jimmy," said Mrs. Collins. "Dale has told us so much about you."

Fidgeting, he didn't know what to say or what to do with his hands. He hoped that Dale hadn't told them too much about him.

Since the two had arrived just as dinner was being put on the table, they all walked into the dining room together.

"Jimmy, you're the guest of honor so you get to sit at the head of the table," said Mr. Collins.

For a brief moment, he felt a little wary of the old man with the gray hair, but he felt safe with everyone together. The family sat down and before he knew it, Dale and Susan reached out and took his hands. Before he could pull back, he noticed everybody was holding hands and Mr. Collins was praying.

"Heavenly father, we thank you for our many blessings, for our health, our home and our country. We especially thank you that our new friend, Jimmy, could be with us today. And finally, we thank you for this food that nourishes

our bodies. In Jesus' name, amen."

Jimmy suddenly had a flashback to his experience with Mr. John when he heard the words, *in Jesus name amen.* He bit his lower lip, taking a deep breath, hoping nobody could see the tears rolling down his cheek.

Everybody started talking at the same time. That, along with the clanging of silverware and clashing of dishes, Jimmy couldn't figure out what to do next. Then Susan picked up his plate and loaded it with some of everything on the table. The food was better than anything he could remember and he was going to eat everything on his plate if it took all night.

When he finally swallowed the last spoonful of cranberry sauce, Mrs. Collins said, "Now for some dessert."

Jimmy didn't think he could possibly eat another bite, but when he saw the pumpkin pie with whipped cream, he couldn't say no.

After dinner, everyone moved to the living room. He sat between Dale and Susan in front of the TV watching the football game. Dale, finding himself getting drowsy, said, "Enough of this watching, let's go outside and play some football ourselves."

For the next hour Jimmy ran out for passes

until Dale's arm gave out and they went back inside, exhausted.

At 6:30 PM, Dale suggested that they better get going if they planned to get back to Shady Hills by eight. For the first time all day, Jimmy's mood turned somber and he quietly began putting on his coat. He knew the day would end, but he wasn't yet ready for it.

It was dark by the time they reached Shady Hills and the motion of the car had put him to sleep. Dale gently woke him and walked him back to the empty pod. The only person there was the one attendant on duty.

As he climbed into bed, Dale said goodbye and promised to see him on Monday. Looking up at Dale in a soft voice he asked, "Dale, can we do this again some time?"

Dale smiled and replied, "Absolutely, Jimmy, I had a great time too."

Dale walked out of the building, tired, but in the best mood, thinking how great the day turned out.

CHAPTER SEVEN

Monday, November 28 at 7:30 AM, Dale walked into Shady Hills in a euphoric mood, looking forward to the week. After scanning the bulletin board for anything new, he checked his message box. A note from Anna Frances told him that Dr. Graves wanted to see him at 9:30 at his Pittsfield office. Dale had not had any contact with Dr. Graves except for a few casual comments in the hall. Anna Frances had always been his go-to person. As Dale was leaving for his appointment with Dr. Graves, he heard Anna's voice from behind him.

"Dale, wait. I need to talk to you before you leave."

"What's up Anna? And what's with Dr. Graves today?"

"I wasn't in my office ten minutes this morning when he called me. He read me the riot act for allowing you to take a patient out of the hospital. So this is just a heads up, you might want to be prepared for a lecture. But don't worry Dale, your job is not in jeopardy, I'll see to that."

"Thanks Anna, I've been on the hot seat before," Dale answered as he headed for the door and the short drive to Pittsfield.

While approaching Dr. Graves' office, he stopped at the secretary's desk.

"Good morning, Mr. Karsten," Elaine greeted him with a smile, "go on in and have a seat, Dr. Graves will be with you shortly."

Dale thanked her and stepped inside, closing the door behind him. The office was well lit thanks to a large picture window looking out into a well-tended flower garden. The décor screamed of ego and self-importance. A huge, mahogany desk was virtually empty except for a monogrammed Mont Blanc pen and pencil set, a black onyx paperweight with gold inlaid initials, and a ceramic coaster with matching coffee mug inscribed with the words, #1 dad.

Behind the desk was a credenza, a perfect match to the desk. Several psychiatric journals neatly fanned out next to a gold-framed picture of a woman and a little girl dressed in equestrian attire, leading a small pony.

On the wall above the credenza was a grouping of diplomas, various awards and certificates, all expertly matted and framed. His brown leather chair more closely resembled a throne, and two smaller matching chairs were placed in front of his desk. The remaining walls were decorated with a collection of Ansell Adams photographs of southwestern landscapes. A putter leaned in the corner next to three Titleist golf balls and a plush deep burgundy carpet would most likely serve him well for practicing his strokes.

The door opened and Dale turned to greet Dr. Graves, who was nearly his own height of 6'2", but thinner with a rangy build. He walked with an arrogant stride and smiled in a condescending manner over his gold rimmed half glasses. Dale judged him to be in his middle forties. His handshake was weak and clammy, but Dr. Graves' eyes pierced right through him.

"Sit down, Mr. Karsten," he said, motioning him toward a chair as he ambled around the big desk and sat down. He wore a gray, cardigan sweater over a white shirt and a burgundy Christian Dior tie, which gave the appearance that he was dressed to color coordinate with his office.

He placed the file he'd been carrying on the desk and Dale immediately recognized the name Simmons, James. Waiting patiently, he noticed Dr. Graves went through a series of mannerisms. He slowly removed his glasses and laid them on Jimmy's file. He leaned back in his chair and pinched the bridge of his nose, feigning stress, or a sinus headache. He placed the file he'd been carrying on the desk and Dale immediately recognized the name Simmons, James. Waiting patiently, he noticed Dr. Graves went through a series of mannerisms. He slowly removed his glasses and laid them on Jimmy's file. He leaned back in his chair and pinched the bridge of his nose, feigning stress, or a sinus headache. Finally, after a moment of meditation, he slowly leaned forward, elbows on his desk, and steepled his fingers together, resembling a spider on a mirror.

"Mr. Karsten," he began, retrieving his glasses and slowly opening the file, "I understand you took a patient home for Thanksgiving, is that right?"

"Yes, I did. I followed all the procedures and filled out all the paperwork in advance."

Glancing down at the file folder, the doctor paused and said, "The subject is James R

Simmons?"

Inwardly Dale seethed and thought, *you obnoxious bastard, his name is Jimmy, not patient, not subject.*

Of course, Dale responded, "Yes."

"Mr. Karsten, how long have you been with us at Shady Hills?"

"It will be two years in February, sir."

"And in two years have you ever taken a patient off the grounds?"

He appeared to be doing a Perry Mason impression, paging through the file pretending to be speed reading.

"No sir, Jimmy was the first."

The doctor peered over his glasses; the word "Jimmy" had not gone unnoticed.

"Mr. Karsten, I've been reading the subject's chart and looking through his file. It appears that you have been spending an inordinate amount of time with him. In fact, isn't it true that you spent off-duty time with the subject?"

"Yes sir, I did."

"Do you ever spend off-duty time with other patients?"

"To this point, no sir, I haven't."

"You have a wife, Mr. Karsten?"

"No sir."

"How about a girlfriend?" He asked again, looking at him over his gold-rimmed reading glasses.

The jerk is insinuating that I'm a pedophile, Dale fumed to himself, resisting the impulse to go over the desk and strangle the pompous bastard.

"Yes, I am engaged," Dale replied, dropping the sir.

Dr. Graves sat massaging his graying temples, eyes closed, as if in deep thought." Mr. Karsten," he began slowly, now looking at the ceiling, "I'm not accusing you of doing anything wrong. In fact, you, no doubt, have good intentions. However, it is my professional opinion that you have allowed yourself to become emotionally involved, which is not in the best interest of you, the child, or the other patients."

"But doctor, the other children have families. This kid has nobody."

"So, you have decided to become his surrogate father or brother?" Graves interrupted in a sarcastic tone.

"No, I haven't decided to be a surrogate father or brother or anything of the sort," Dale replied, trying to keep his emotions in check.

"Well, what then?"

"I don't know, perhaps a friend, confidant, a sounding board. This child has nobody."

The doctor again steepled his fingers, now looking more like a Supreme Court Justice than a psychiatrist. "Mr. Karsten, I am director of all the mental health facilities in this region, and I'm responsible for the welfare of all the people, the patients, attendants, custodians, cooks and bottle washers. I make hard decisions every day." He paused for effect before continuing. "It is my decision that it is not in your or the patient's best interest for this relationship to continue. Consequently, you are being transferred to pod seven to work with the fourteen and sixteen-year old boys."

"Please sir," Dale began, but was quickly interrupted.

"That's my decision, Mr. Karsten; it is not negotiable. Or, if you wish, we can request your transfer to another facility; perhaps to Pittsfield State Hospital. Think about that."

Rising from his chair, the doctor looked at his watch, signaling that the meeting was indeed over. Dale stood without comment and started toward the door.

"Mr. Karsten, you are to report to pod seven this morning."

"But doctor, could I at least," he began.

"It's irrevocable, Mr. Karsten. I've made my decision, is that clear?"

Without answering, Dale wheeled around and walked out of the office. Walking back to his car, he said, "Looks like I have some decisions to make."

CHAPTER EIGHT

When Jimmy woke on Monday morning, there was a new attendant on duty in his pod, a guy named Mr. Fetzer. "Where is Dale, er, I mean Mr. Karsten?"

"I don't know, but you better get ready for school."

Feeling sudden panic, he thought, *No, not again, something bad is going to happen; I just know it. He did something wrong, or said something wrong to Mr. and Mrs. Collins; why am I so stupid?*

"Jimmy," said Mr. Fetzer, "are you all right?"

"Where is Dale?"

"I've already told you; I don't know. Now you need to get ready for school. Mr. Karsten will probably be here when you get back."

He immediately seized on that statement. Yes, he'll be here when I get back. He wouldn't leave me, we're friends.

When Dale showed up at Pod seven, Pete Fetzer was gathering his personal belongings. 'Looks like you and I are trading places for a while," Pete said.

"Yeah, it looks that way," Dale said with a resigned sigh, not wanting to discuss the whys and wherefores at the moment.

"Pete, would you do me a favor?"

"Sure, Dale, if I can."

"Did you meet Jimmy Simmons this morning?"

"Yes, you mean that little kid that kept asking about you?"

"Jimmy is rather special. He was born at Pittsfield State Hospital. He has no family, never gets any visitors, and could use a little special attention."

Pete looked a bit bewildered, but shrugged and said, "Sure Dale, no problem. See you later."

Dale settled into the chair in his new office, leaned back with his hands laced behind his head, eyes closed, still trying to make sense out of everything. He looked around pod seven, which was exactly the same layout as the other pods. The kids would be in school for the next few hours, so Dale began reading the charts of his 14 to 16-year-old patients.

After completing four charts and having retained little or nothing at all, he dropped his pencil on the desk, shoving the files aside. He sat there, replaying the conversation with Graves, when it occurred to him. Nobody said he couldn't pick up his belongings, which might give him a chance to explain things to Jimmy.

After school, Dale still had not shown up before all the children were taken outside for recreation. Jimmy refused to join the others in soccer, but instead sat alone on the Jungle Jim. I must be a real bad person, Jimmy thought. Mrs. Barnes always said, Jesus loves the little children, and if you are good you will be blessed and you will be happy. I'm not good, that's why Mr. Barnes did the bad thing to me, and that's why Dale went away. Bad kids never have a real home like the kids on T.V.

Jimmy looked up to see Dale walking toward him. His heart dropped, when he noticed the serious expression on Dale's face. Something must be terribly wrong.

"Hi Jimmy," Dale said noticing he would not make eye contact.

He didn't look up, but continued to stare at

the ground.

"Jimmy," Dale began, "I was late today because Dr. Graves, my supervisor, called me to his office."

"So?" He said still not wanting to look up.

"Dr. Graves called me to his office this morning to tell me I was being transferred."

"To another pod?"

"Maybe, or to another hospital, I'm not sure yet. I don't want to leave you and the other children. Maybe it won't be too long, and in a few months, I could be transferred back here."

Jimmy closed his eyes tight, clenching his fists as Dale was talking. "I don't believe you," he cried. "I hate you."

"Jimmy, you don't mean that."

"I had a rotten time at Thanksgiving. I hate those people too."

"Jimmy, I know how you feel, and . . . "

"You don't know anything, you're just like everybody else." He kicked out, barely missing Dale, then ran away screaming, "I hate you. I hate you."

Dale stood motionless as two other attendants chased him down and carried him, screaming, back to his pod. He broke loose momentarily and began throwing chairs and turning over tables. The attendants again wrestled him to his bed and held him down.

"No, no, please don't do the bad thing, oh god, please."

He felt the sting of the hypodermic needle in his buttocks, then relaxed, sobbing into his pillow. He felt someone pull his pants up and roll him onto his back. Things were getting fuzzy, but he also began to feel better. He felt the leather straps tighten around his wrists and ankles, but didn't care. He no longer cared about anything as he closed his eyes and waited for all the pain to go away.

As Dale was leaving the hospital, he met Anna walking towards him.

"Dale," she said, "seems that news travels fast. I just got an irate phone call from Dr. Graves. I explained to him that you went to get your personal belongings while Jimmy was at school and inadvertently ran into him. Don't worry, it doesn't rise to the level of insubordination. But tell me, Dale, between you and me, you were hoping to see Jimmy," she said with a sly grin. I'm sorry it didn't work out."

* * *

Over time, Dale became accustomed to the

older boys and his duties in pod seven. He knew jumping from ages 10 through 11 to 15 and 16 years of age was going to be a challenge. His friend Pete kept him up to date regarding Jimmy's progress, which was very little at this time.

Dale stood in the lunch room trying to decide where to sit, when his friend Pete Fetzer waved him over where a group of attendants were sitting at a large round table. Two people at the table were transfers from Pittsfield. Pete introduced Dale to Robbie Patterson and Jim Jenkins.

"These two guys decided to move over to the good side of town," Pete said jokingly. Dale shook both their hands as they all sat down. Conversation seemed to go in all directions when the young man, Robbie Patterson said, "I hear Rachel Simmons' kid is in here."

This immediately caught Dale's attention.

"You know Rachel Simmons, James Simmons' mother?"

"Well, I don't know her, but I do know about her. Her son, James, was conceived by rape in her room as the story goes. She actually had twins, at least that's what I've been told."

"Was there any kind of investigation by outside law enforcement?" Dale asked.

"None that I know of," Robbie said. Dr. Graves interviewed everybody who was on staff that night. A maintenance man reported that the screen on her window appeared to be tampered with. Everybody assumed that a male patient broke into her room that night."

"Assumed," Dale said with a cynical chuckle, "you know what they say about people who assume."

"No," said Robbie "what do they say about people who assume?"

"It makes an ass of you and me. It sounds like the Keystone cops would have done a better job. There should have been a thorough investigation, both internal and by outside law enforcement," Dale said, shaking his head. "Whether it's federal, state or local, there's the right way, the wrong way, and the government way." Dale glanced at his watch, stood up and shook hands with the two new guys." Gotta get back to work," he said as he walked away, still shaking his head.

Dale made a final entry in one of the boy's charts, placed it in the file drawer and turned to leave when his phone rang.

"Mr. Karsten, this is Dr. Graves. It's been

brought to my attention that you do not approve of my methods in running this institution. First you become personally involved with the minor patient, now it has been reported that you've been inquiring about his mother, who is a patient here at Pittsfield. What's your fascination with this family?"

"Dr. Graves, I was simply sitting at lunch when one of my colleagues mentioned Jimmy's mother was raped in her room. It was just a casual conversation. I was curious as to how it could happen and, if so, had the rapist been charged with the crime?"

"Mr. Karsten, you seem to have a habit of getting involved in matters that don't concern you, and quite frankly, it's beginning to be a distraction. It's my job to investigate the Rachel Simmons case, and every other situation. It's your job to follow orders and adhere to proper protocol. If you have a desire to be a detective, I'm sure the County Sheriff's office could use a gifted sleuth like you."

"But doctor," Dale began.

"But nothing, Mr. Karsten," Dr. Graves interrupted. "You are precariously close to disciplinary action. Do I make myself clear?"

"Disciplinary action for what, Dr. Graves?"

"Insubordination for one thing, and meddling outside the realm of your responsibilities."

"May I explain?" Dale began.

"No, you may not," Graves said in an angry tone. "Read your job description and perform your duties accordingly," he said hanging up the phone.

As Dale drove home, he replayed in his mind the conversation with Dr. Graves. Remembering the conversation at lunch, it became obvious to Dale that Robbie Patterson was a mole planted at Shady Hills by Graves to keep him up to speed on everything and everyone. The idea that what he shared in confidence was immediately reported to the administrator infuriated him. In his current frame of mind Dale realized that he would not be very good company to anybody this evening.

When he arrived home, he called Susan and told her he didn't feel well and wouldn't be coming over. She sensed something was troubling him, but thought this was not the time to press the issue. Dale was grateful for her intuition and promised to see her tomorrow. He threw a Swanson dinner in the oven out of habit, but realized he had no appetite. Twisting the cap off a Budweiser, he sat down in his big green

La-Z-Boy to consider his options.

It crossed his mind to tell Dr. Graves and the State of Ohio to go straight to hell, but considering his new responsibilities that would come with marriage and a family, his common sense kicked in. Maybe he should consider Pittsfield State Hospital, since his rank of Phys-Aid III would remain intact. Adult patients would eliminate the risk of becoming emotionally involved. On the other hand, he loved his job at Shady Hills, working with kids who for the most part can be helped, versus custodial care to the infirmed. Although a noble undertaking, it offered less personal satisfaction. Also to be considered was the extra thirty-minute round trip, an additional two hours per week behind the wheel. The thought of working in the same building under the watchful eye of Dr. Graves made him shudder.

His thoughts were interrupted when he suddenly smelled smoke. Looking up, he saw smoke pouring from the oven door. Dale ran, turned off the oven, grabbed two potholders and dumped what no longer resembled meatloaf into the sink while turning on the water. As he began opening the apartment windows, the phone rang. The instant he heard his mother's voice, he knew there was something wrong.

"Dale, it's Dad," she said.

"What is it Mom, is Dad sick?"

"No honey, he's. . . he's gone." With that, she broke down, sobbing uncontrollably.

Dale waited a moment then said, "Mom, what do you mean gone? Gone where?"

"He was late for dinner. He was in the barn working and when he didn't come in, I went looking for him. Dale, I found him lying on the path between the pump house and the silo. I called for help and when the ambulance came, they tried everything they could, but he's gone. Dale, what am I going to do?"

"I'm coming home, mom, I'll be there first thing in the morning. Is there anybody with you?"

"Aunt Carol is on her way. She should be here in a few minutes." With that, her sobbing continued.

"Go ahead mom, it's okay to cry," Dale said, having a difficult time holding his own tears back.

"That's the doorbell," his mother said. "Aunt Carol is here."

"Good, I'll see you in the morning, I love you, Mom."

As if in a fog, Dale gathered some toiletries and clothes and stuffed it all into his suitcase for the trip, then called Susan. Susan answered on the first ring. She sat shaking in total disbelief as Dale told her about his mother's phone call.

" I'm leaving about 6 o'clock tomorrow morning," he said.

"And I will be at your apartment at six to go with you," she answered.

"Are you sure, honey? What about your job?"

"Don't worry about my job, I've accumulated enough sick time and personal time. I'm coming. I don't want you to be alone."

CHAPTER 9

The church was packed with friends and family. Dale and Mrs. Karsten dutifully accepted the expressions of sympathy from the seemingly endless line of friends. After the gravesite services, the three of them went back to the big farmhouse where Dale grew up.

He stood in his familiar room that night looking out at the barn surrounded by 600 acres of rolling pastureland gone dormant as Indian summer surrendered to the intrusion of winter. He longed to be ten years old again, to run carefree through those fields, to walk across the beam high up in the barn, pretending to walk the tightrope in a circus act, only to fall into the hay below.

The smell of hay momentarily invaded his senses. There are no soft places to fall when you grow up, he mused. He was responsible for the farm now; his mother couldn't handle it.

His options had narrowed. Soon he would have to move back home. First, he hoped Susan would agree to change their wedding date and settle for a scaled-down private ceremony.

Dale and Susan remained at the farm another week putting his father's affairs in order. Insurance policies, payroll for the farmhands, and putting his dad's longtime friend and most trusted employee, Walt Kaiser, in charge of the day-to-day operations. He also arranged for his uncle Harold and aunt Carol to stop by on a regular basis to check up on his mother.

As they drove away, Dale watched his childhood home shrink into the distance through his rearview mirror. His mind was flooded with memories of his father and all the things they did together, like 4-H projects and quail hunting. Looking over at Susan, who was leaning back in the seat with her eyes closed, Dale finally spoke.

"What are you thinking about, Suzie Q?"

She opened her eyes, turned toward him and replied, "I was just about to ask you the same question."

Smiling, Dale said, "Ok, you go first."

"Well, I was thinking about how serene and peaceful the farm is. The fresh country air, the smell of new-mown hay. The beautiful sunrise coming over the tree-lined mountains and setting behind that big, red barn. Even the sounds of the farm animals had a soothing effect on me. Your family and friends were so warm and friendly, treating me like I was already a member of the family. How could you have ever left that place?"

"I guess I just took it for granted, but listening to you now makes me appreciate it in a whole new way."

"Now it's your turn Dale. What were you thinking about?"

He took a deep breath and let out a long sigh of relief. "You're not going to believe this," he said, "but I've been agonizing over the subject of possibly moving back to the farm. I've been racking my brain, rehearsing in my mind exactly how I might convince you. You'll never know how thrilled I am right now to hear you say how much you love it. You have definitely made my day."

"Honey, my parents always told me that a happy marriage isn't a place, a big fancy home, or lots of money. A happy marriage is two people who love each other and spend a life together. That's all I want for us."

"While we're on the subject of marriage," Dale replied with a sly grin, "that is another subject that I have been worrying about the last few days."

"Don't tell me you're backing out," she said in a joking manner, but still a little taken back.

"Backing out? I can't imagine living the rest of my life without you. I know every woman dreams of their wedding day, and how they plan everything from their wedding gowns to bride's maids, to the reception. I also know that you have been looking forward to our honeymoon."

"Yes, go on," she said.

"Well, considering what we've been through this last couple of weeks, I was wondering if you might settle for a scaled-down private wedding with family and a few close friends. When things settle down, we can take that trip to Niagara Falls, just like we've planned." Dale paused, not knowing how to continue, when he felt her hand on his shoulder. Looking over at her he saw tears streaming down her face.

"We are so much on the same page that it's scary," she said through her tears.

"I have been thinking exactly the same thing, with all the emotional turmoil that we've been through, the death of your dad, changing jobs and moving to another state would have such a negative effect on us. We wouldn't be able to enjoy the honeymoon under that much stress."

At that moment Dale turned into a rest area.

"Why are you stopping?" she asked.

While tearing up himself, Dale simply said, "Because, I need a hug." Pulling into the first vacant spot, they held each other for several minutes. Finally, Dale said, "Susan, you are the most beautiful, understanding woman I have ever met, and I love you more than you'll ever know. Let's stop at the next exit, have some lunch, and plan our future."

"Exactly what I was thinking," she said, laughing. "See, we're on the same page again."

They arrived home early that afternoon. It was a beautiful sunny day. Neither was in the mood to cook, so they had a fast food dinner at a little place called the Kwik Shake. When they arrived at Susan's apartment, Dale sat behind the wheel, leaning back with his arms folded across his chest, as if lost in thought. Susan sat looking at him for a moment. "Penny for your thoughts," she said, slowly removing her sunglasses.

"I was just thinking, this time next month there will no longer be your place and my place, just our place. I can't wait."

"Now, that thought is worth far more than a penny. In fact, it's priceless. Let's go in and have a glass of wine and relax."

"You come up with some of the best ideas," Dale said as he retrieved her suitcase from the backseat. "Lead the way, my lady," he said with a slight bow and a sweeping hand gesture toward the door.

* * *

When Dale entered Anna Frances' office Monday morning, she came around her desk and gave him a warm hug. "I'm so sorry about your loss," she said. "I lost my father two years ago and I know how you feel. If there's anything we can do, time off to deal with family issues, anything at all." She held him at arm's length, look into his eyes and said, "Dale, you are the shining star around here. We appreciate everything you do."

Smiling appreciatively, Dale replied, "You're making the reason for my visit very difficult."

"Oh, and how is that?" she asked with a puzzled expression.

"Well, I can't tell you how much I love this job. I really felt like I had found my purpose, but," he said while searching for the right words.

"But?" Anna repeated.

Pausing again, Dale said, "A six hundred-acre dairy farm cannot run itself and my mother could never handle the job alone. Of course, we have hired hands, but they could not deal with the business end of the farm; this needs a family member, and being the only child, the responsibility falls on me." Dale paused, trying to find the right words.

"Dale," Anna said while holding up her hands in a stop gesture. "I totally understand that you have to leave. Everybody here will miss you, including Jimmy. Lately he's been asking about you."

"That's surprising, as the last time he saw me, he said he hated me!"

"After he quieted down, and Jimmy was in a listening mood, Pete Fetzer explained that the situation was not what you wanted or could control. Jimmy seemed to accept it, however, he still has a way to go. Some days his anger is so out of control that it frightens the other boys."

"Dr. Graves was right about me," Dale replied. "I was getting too involved with Jimmy, but I had this feeling that I was all he had and was the only person who understood him."

"Dale, like it or not, you were the only father figure he had, even though it was only for a short time. Maybe with the proper treatment, we can purge his demons. It would help if we knew who his father was. He has a twin brother who, unlike Jimmy, was very healthy at birth. He was adopted by a family from out of state. Unfortunately, nobody knows exactly where he is today. We know that his mother, before her accident, was highly intelligent.

"We'll miss you, Dale, but try not to dwell on the past." Anna then added, "If you ever feel that farming is not your life-long vocation, there will always be a position for you here."

The next several days proved beyond hectic. Anna Frances surprised Dale with a farewell party at a small pub called the Brandywine Tavern. Dale was overwhelmed at the number of people who showed up to give their condolences and wish him well. It was a bittersweet day to say the least. Dale knew he would miss working with the kids, but his responsibilities to his mother and the family farm had to be his number one priority.

Dale and Susan stayed busy with a myriad of details required before moving. Things like canceling electric, telephone, bank accounts and trash removal. Dale fortunately found someone to sublet his apartment that had approximately a year left on his lease. Susan's lease, however, was about to expire in another month. Since his dad's pickup truck was less than a year old with very low mileage, Dale placed an ad in the local paper and sold his VW beetle. Finally, with all the mundane chores out of the way, they were free to plan their wedding and move on together.

* * *

Mrs. Collins made arrangements for the wedding at the First Methodist Church of Ashland, the same church where she and her husband took their vows. Their pastor, Charles Martin, came out of retirement to officiate the wedding. Mr. and Mrs. Collins and Mary Karsten together walked the bride down the aisle. Susan was a picture to behold in her simple ivory-beaded dress. Dale's emotions were heartfelt as he struggled for composure as the service started. By the time it was his turn to say his vows, Dale repeated them in a strong, confident voice.

The reception was held in a private room at a

popular restaurant called The Wine Cellar. The evening was a complete success with great food, music and dancing. At one point during the mother-son dance, Dale's mother looked up at him with teary eyes, "I wish your dad was here right now. I miss him so much," then added, "he would be so proud of you. I know he met Susan once during your short visit, but many times he said what a perfect match she was for you."

Dale gently lifted her chin and smiled down at her. "Thanks Mom. Dad is here with us; I can feel his presence. We just can't see him, but one day we will."

The best man, Dale's friend from high school, and the bridesmaid, Susan's long- time friend and neighbor, gave a short speech along with a toast. After many well-wishers and hugs, Mr. Collins then presented them with the key to the bridal suite at a well-known resort, the Valley View Inn. Dodging a barrage of rice, the newlyweds ran to their car and drove away to the clanging sound of tin cans that someone had tied to the back of their car.

After a wonderful weekend at the Valley View Inn, the hard work lay ahead. Dale and Susan spent the week packing and sorting through what they planned to take and what was going to be sold or donated. On moving day, they drove away in Susan's Chevy Impala, pulling a U-Haul Trailer, going east on Interstate 80 toward Luthersburg, Pennsylvania, a small farming community.

* * *

Susan adapted to country living like she was born into it. She planted a vegetable garden and tried her hand at raising some chickens. She and Mrs. Karsten became a team as Mrs. Karsten taught her how to can fruits and vegetables in glass Mason jars. Susan's strawberry jam actually won a third-place ribbon at the county fair. Before long, it was natural for Susan to refer to her as "Mom."

On the other hand, Dale picked up where he left off. His dad had taught him well. His laid-back, peaceful attitude, however, was often invaded by memories of Jimmy Simmons and that Thanksgiving Day. It haunted him constantly. He missed the joy he had felt working with the boys. Several times he had the impulse to call Shady Hills, but changed his mind. What could he do anyway? Best to leave that part of his life behind him and concentrate on the farm and the family.

The following year, Susan gave birth to a healthy baby boy. They named him Dale Junior, but soon he acquired the nickname DJ.

Running the farm 24 hours a day, seven days a week left little time for vacations. At best they were limited to weekend day trips.

Five years later, Mrs. Karsten remarried a widower who attended the same church. Her new husband, Bill Marshall, was an old friend of Dale's father. They volunteered to run the farm for a couple of weeks so Dale and his family could go on a real vacation.

CHAPTER TEN

On a bright July morning Dale, Susan and six-year-old DJ, set out for a week's vacation to visit Susan's parents back in Ohio. Dale played golf with Mr. Collins, visited some old friends and generally relaxed. On the third day, torrential rains kept them inside and on an impulse Dale decided to call Shady Hills.

"Anna Frances, please," he said to the receptionist.

She picked up on the first ring. "Administration, this is Anna."

"And this is a blast from the past," Dale said upon hearing her familiar voice.

"Dale, what a surprise! Where are you?"

"I'm at my in-laws house about eighty miles south of you, and I was wondering if you would be available for lunch tomorrow."

She opened her day planner and said, "Yes, I'd love to have lunch with you, but I'm a bit short-staffed. Could we meet here in the cafeteria?"

"The cafeteria is fine with me. I'll see you around noon."

Dale stood in the doorway of the cafeteria scanning the room when he saw the familiar face of Anna as she waved to him. He walked over to the far corner where she was sitting, both were smiling as they hugged each other.

"You don't know how nice it is to see you again, Dale. The staff is constantly asking if I've heard from you. I don't think you realize the lasting impact you've had on the people here." With all the excitement, neither of them appeared to be very hungry, so Dale went to the serving line and returned with two cups of coffee. They talked and reminisced about everything except the real reason for Dale's visit.

Anna folded her arms, leaned back and with uncanny perception, came right to the point. "You want to know what's become of Jimmy Simmons, am I right?"

After an uncomfortable pause, Dale answered, "As a matter of fact, I do."

She looked down, grimaced and shook her head. Finishing her last bit of coffee, she slowly laid the cup aside. She responded with the absolute last words Dale wanted to hear.

"After you left, he went straight downhill. No-body could get close to him. He became angry and argumentative. He was a hopeless case. The staff could hardly wait for his 16th birthday, at which time he was transferred to Pittsfield. As far as I know, he's still there. Dale. For what it's worth, everybody here agrees that you could have and would have helped that boy."

"I appreciate the kind words Anna. It's too bad Dr. Graves didn't share the same opinion. And while we're on the subject of Dr. Graves and Pittsfield, I might just drop in there before I head back to Ashland."

"I hope you know what you're doing. If Graves gets wind of your visit, I have no idea how he'll react."

"Don't worry, the last time I looked, Pitts-field was a state-run facility paid for by we, the taxpayers."

"But Dale, are you forgetting that you are no longer a resident of the State of Ohio, therefore, you pay no taxes?"

"Then I guess I'll just have to take my chances. I've come too far to leave without some closure."

With that Dale stood to leave. "I've enjoyed

our visit and we should do this more often. I'm sure my wife Susan would love to see you as well."

"That would be nice Dale, I'll look forward to it. Well, I've gotta get back to work, you take care and please keep in touch." After a brief hug, she walked Dale to the door before turning back toward her office.

* * *

Dale stepped outside into the rain, not really looking forward to his next destination, Pittsfield Psychiatric Hospital on the outskirts of Cleveland.

The reception area was deserted except for a middle-aged woman who appeared behind a long counter. "Can I help you, sir?" she said looking over her reading glasses and pushing a Nora Roberts novel aside.

"Yes ma'am, I'm inquiring about a patient, Jimmy or James Simmons."

At the mention of James Simmons, her friendly expression turned to one of suspicion. "Are you a relative?" she asked.

"No, I guess you could say I'm a friend."

"I'm sorry sir, but I'm afraid you'll have to come back another time. Perhaps talk to one of the doctors." She was now a little agitated, anxious to end the conversation.

"Look ma'am, I worked at Shady Hills Hospital for children several years ago and you might say I took special interest in Jimmy. I only want to know if he's all right. I live in Pennsylvania now and will be going back in a few days. I'm just inquiring as to his welfare."

He noticed the woman had relaxed somewhat. She looked around, like people do before telling an ethnic joke. Satisfied that they were alone, she beckoned Dale closer.

"You didn't hear this from me," she began. "When the young man, James Simmons, was transferred here, being the youngest at only sixteen, he became the target of the older patients. By the time he was eighteen, the bullying was unbearable. It seems that Mr. Simmons was forced into fight or flight mode. One day, a particularly sadistic patient decided to take the dessert from his tray. This pushed him to the limit and he knocked his tormentor unconscious with a chair. By the time the attendants got there the patient was lying on the floor and still not moving. Fortunately, he was not seriously injured, just a mild concussion. Dr. Graves considered it a violent attack and ordered Mr. Simmons to be relocated to Bainbridge State Hospital."

"Bainbridge?" Dale asked with astonishment. "Bainbridge State Hospital for the criminally insane?"

"Yes, I'm afraid so," she said in a shaky voice. "I have to tell you, most of the staff did not believe he was violent and thought the transfer was totally undeserved."

Dale could not believe what he'd heard, or imagined Jimmy doing such a thing. Bainbridge State Hospital was known as the Alcatraz of mental institutions in the State of Ohio. He stood speechless and turned to leave.

"Sir," the woman said, "remember, you didn't hear that from me."

He was in such a state of mind, he didn't hear a word she said. In fact, he didn't even remember the drive back to his family and Ashland.

That night he sat with Susan outside on the patio and went over every detail of his conversation with Anna and what he learned at Pittsfield. Susan remained silent, letting her husband talk about Bainbridge State Hospital.

"Jimmy won't come out of that house of horrors alive. I've heard about that place. Based on what I've heard, no human being should be there." At times, Dale appeared to be rambling, making no sense to her, but she listened until he had nothing more to say.

Susan got up and walked behind Dale's chair and began to gently rub his shoulders. "Honey," she said, "I can't imagine how you feel; but you have a life and family here. You've done everything humanly possible for that young man. More than anybody else. The way you pay attention to little DJ tells me that you've learned an awful lot about how to deal with children. There's nothing more you can do except try and put it behind you. We need you, all four of us."

"Four?" Dale asked. "Mom's remarried, so it's just you, me and DJ."

"Honey, I was going to save this surprise until we were all together tomorrow evening at dinner, but you need something else to think about. Something good for a change. This time next year, DJ is gonna have a brother or sister."

"Oh my God, are you kidding me!" he exclaimed, jumping up and taking her in his arms. "You don't know how happy that makes me. You're so right, I need to concentrate on making the main thing the main thing. And the main thing is our family."

Dale held her at arm's length, smiling broadly for the first time since he got home.

"We'll tell the family tomorrow. The weather has cleared up and dad made a tee time for both of you tomorrow morning at 7 o'clock."

After a day on the golf course, where Dale shot the worst round of golf in recent memory, he blamed his poor score on lack of concentration.

That evening, Susan's family, along with some relatives and close family friends, enjoyed an incredible meal prepared by Mrs. Collins. The highlight of the evening came when Susan stood up, raised her glass of wine and said, "I have an announcement to make." The room went quiet in expectation. "I would like to propose a toast," she said. When they all raised their glasses, she paused for dramatic effect. "Here's to our new baby, who is expected to arrive in early February." The room erupted with applause and cheers. Mr. and Mrs. Collins could scarcely contain themselves.

"Yes," Mr. Collins joked holding his class high. "I'm going to have another golfing buddy, and I certainly hope he plays a better game than his dad." This brought a round of laughter from everybody, including Dale.

"Not so fast, Grandpa. I'm hoping you're going to get a granddaughter!"

After dessert, the guests began to leave, but not before everyone congratulated Dale and Susan on the news of their expected addition to the family.

Thirty minutes into their trip home, DJ fell asleep in the back seat as Susan sat leafing through a magazine called Motherhood, while Dale said nothing since they left.

Laying her magazine aside, Susan turned toward Dale and remarked, "You know how I often ask you what you're thinking?"

"Yes honey, you ask me that a lot."

"Well, I don't have to ask you this time, because I know what you're thinking. You're thinking about that young boy, Jimmy. I believe you've been preoccupied with his situation since your visit to the hospital."

"You're so perceptive, it's scary," Dale admitted. "I can't believe what's happened to him, or that he could actually beat somebody with a chair. The Jimmy I knew was somewhat timid and I'd never seen him become aggressive. Well no, he did go pretty ballistic and actually kicked me when I told him I was being relocated. But a ten-year-old lashing out isn't the same as an eighteen-year old hitting someone with a chair. Now he is being incarcerated in a hell hole they call a hospital. It's more like a zoo. There are stories of patients being beaten, raped and even killed by the staff. I know there's nothing I can do for him; in fact, I'm convinced that he's probably a lost cause. I just can't get it out of my head."

Neither spoke for a short time. Dale was mentally forming his next remark. "You know honey, I've been thinking about something. I'm considering professional counseling. I can't be the kind of father and husband that you and DJ deserve, if I don't put this whole thing behind me. I'm going to speak with Pastor Bruce. Maybe he can suggest someone."

"If getting some counseling would make you feel better, I'm all for it. Whatever you do, remember, I'm with you all the way. We'll get through this together."

"I'm going to speak with pastor Bruce after church on Sunday. Now, let's talk about something more pleasant."

"Okay, what do you want to talk about? I know what I would like to talk about."

"And what would that be?"

"We need to decide what we're going to name our new baby."

"Hmm," Dale said. "I've been thinking about that myself. If it's a boy, I've narrowed it down to Clem, Gus or Festus. If it's a girl, I would like to name her Gladys or Gertrude."

"You are not serious!" Susan said, unable to stop laughing. "That is so funny."

"Well, I decided we needed a little levity."

Both sat quietly running names through their mind. Susan was the first to speak.

"I've been thinking about names since I found out I was pregnant. If it's a boy, I'd like to name him Jason. If it's a girl, I think Sarah is a beautiful name."

"Jason Karsten, Sarah Karsten." Dale repeated out loud. "They both have a nice ring to it; but I'm still partial to Clem and Gertrude.'

"Stop it," she said, punching him in the shoulder. "You are such a silly goose, but I love you."

Reaching over and gently patting her knee, Dale answered, "I love you too and I think Jason and Sarah are really nice names."

They spent the rest of the trip discussing everything from their visit to preparing a room for the baby. As they pulled off the main road and onto the gravel driveway, the crunching sound brought DJ out of a sound sleep. They both agreed that it was an enjoyable trip, but it was always nice to get home.

CHAPTER 11

"You must be Mr. Karsten," said the tall, middle-aged woman as she met Dale halfway across the reception area, giving him a warm handshake. She was wearing a casual, gray pants suit and her hair was tied back in a tight bun. Her jeweled reading glasses were hanging from a gold chain around her neck.

As they walked together, Dale remarked, "Pastor Bruce Kern highly recommended Dr. Hansen as an outstanding Christian counselor."

"That he is, he has an excellent reputation. Follow me please." She led him down a hallway to a small room furnished with a couch and two overstuffed chairs, surrounding an ornate mahogany coffee table. Under it was a beautiful Persian rug. A small sidebar contained a silver tray with matching coffeepot and ornate ceramic mugs.

While Dale was admiring a collage of artwork by Margaret Keane, the artist famous for painting children with enormous eyes, a voice behind him said, "Good morning, Dale."

Turning, he came face-to-face with a man about his own height who looked to be approximately sixty years old. He had deep blue eyes, curly gray hair, a friendly smile and a firm handshake.

"I'm Dr. Hansen," he said, "but everybody calls me Doc. How about some coffee?" he asked, reaching for the pot.

"I would love some coffee, please, black is fine."

Dr. Hansen sat down in the chair next to Dale, remarking about their fantastic weather. "Pastor Bruce tells me you were one of his favorite kids in youth group. He said you were always compassionate and willing to help any of the younger kids fit in."

"Well, Doc, sometimes too much compassion can be hurtful, which is why I'm here today".

"Tell me, Dale, what makes you say that?"

"It started about six years ago when I was working as a psych aid at Shady Hills Hospital for emotionally disturbed children. There was this kid named Jimmy who was born to a mental patient. His mother, who is in a vegetative state, was raped one evening.

Nobody knows who the father is, so most people presume he was also mentally deficient. Consequently, he was always overlooked by adopting parents. He spent time in several foster homes. For one reason or another, none of them worked out.

I met him when he was admitted to Shady Hills. I saw something in him, and felt all he needed was some special attention. I took it upon myself to work with him. I even checked him out of the hospital one Thanksgiving and took him to my in-law's home. We hiked, visited a petting zoo that day, and even played catch with a football. Jimmy was as normal as any kid I've ever known.

"My actions got me on the wrong side of the hospital administrator, Dr. Graves. He decided that it would be in the best interest of everybody if I were moved to a different location. Unfortunately, my father died shortly thereafter and I moved back to the farm."

Like a good counselor, Dr. Hansen listened intently, then said, "Go on."

"My family and I recently took a short vacation in Ashland, Ohio, which is only about 80 miles from Shady Hills. One day on impulse I drove there hoping to see how Jimmy was doing. I learned from a friend of mine that he had digressed to the point where they admitted him to Pittsfield State. I'm told he had an altercation with another patient and beat him with a wooden chair. The patient survived and Jimmy, only eighteen years old, was sent to Bainbridge Psychiatric Hospital for the criminally insane.

"I'm here, Doctor, because I can't get it off my mind. I believe I could've helped him. I should have done more. I was his only friend." Dale's voice was shaking and a tear rolled down his cheek as he tried to hold his emotions back.

Dr. Hansen handed him a tissue, saying, "Here, please continue."

"The situation haunts me continuously to the point where I'm afraid it's going to take a toll on my family. How can I purge this nightmare?"

Dr. Hansen reached over, placed his hand on Dale's shoulder, and looked him straight in the eyes. "Dale, yours is not an uncommon problem. It's called rumination syndrome."

"Ruma what?" he asked. "Is it treatable?"

"You're a dairy farmer, so I'm sure you will understand what I'm talking about. Tell me Dale, what do cows do?

"Well, they give milk" he replied.

"What else?"

"They walk around all day eating grass."

"They eat grass, what else do they do?"

"Well, they just stand around chewing their cud."

"Bingo," Dr. Hansen said in a victorious tone. "The word rumination comes from the word ruminate. Ruminate derives from *ruminari,* that's the Latin name for the first stomach compartment of ruminant animals, like cows. So, the cow munches on grass and chews and chews and chews some more. The cow finally swallows the grass and in a little while regurgitates it back up and chews some more. They continue to do this all day. They ruminate, which is good for the cow. However, we have people who are mental ruminators. They think about an unhappy experience in their life for a while. They put it out of their mind, only to regurgitate the memory and the process starts all over. What you need to do, Dale, is spit out the cud."

"How do I do that?"

"It's a simple two-step formula; number one, distract. Absorb yourself in a different activity, essentially stopping the rumination and spitting out that yucky, regurgitated mental cud.

"The next step occurs while you are doing something different. You want to engage all five senses and hyper-focus your attention on what you are doing in that moment. Experts call it mindfulness. Concentrate on a pleasant experience. Tell me Dale, what is one of the most pleasant experiences of your life?"

"Wow, there's been so many. The first time I looked into my wife's eyes and knew we were meant to be together. The day I held my son in my arms for the first time was an experience I'll never forget."

"That's what I'm talking about. You need to overpower the negative with positive thoughts like that. Another excellent distraction is interaction with your son. What are some of the things your son enjoys?"

"Last weekend, I watched his grandmother reading him a book about an elephant. He smiled continuously through the story. Perhaps I could carve out a little time every evening and read to him. What would you suggest?"

"Children seem to love Dr. Seuss; The Cat in the Hat, Green Eggs and Ham, that sort of thing would be a good place to start. What other distraction can you think of?"

"I've been thinking about volunteering. My

church has a soup kitchen. They collect items for the homeless. I think I'd like to do something like that. Also, my wife enjoys the occasional date night, a dinner out and a movie. We don't do that enough and I think it's about time to make it a weekly event."

"What else can you think of?"

"My son has been wanting to build a tree house like his friend Caleb has, but I keep putting it off. That is also going to change. Don't you think that would be a good father and son project?"

"Well, it certainly sounds like you have enough distractions to swallow that cud or spit it out."

"Doc, this seems so simple, and easy to do, I just never took the time to find a solution. I should've been speaking to somebody like you for the last several years. I believe that you may have given me the answer and I thank you."

"One last question, Dr. Hansen. Do you think that because the situation with Jimmy was so painful for me that I have been subconsciously putting distance between my own family?"

"Well, that is hard to say, but you may have a point. The important thing is you are asking the right questions and are implementing a plan.

You're going into this with the right attitude and I'm sure you'll be successful. But, remember, I'm here anytime you want to talk."

As Dale stood up, Dr. Hansen walked him to the door. Shaking his hand, he said, "Say hello to Pastor Bruce and remember, I'm here if you need me."

CHAPTER 12

Dale was watching the sun set while relaxing on his porch thinking that it'd been six years since his visit with Dr. Hansen, and he'd never been happier. The demon had been exercised. It was hard to believe that DJ was now 11 and active in 4H as well as Cub Scouts. He proudly showed off the blue ribbon he won for a steer he raised from a calf. He laughed out loud thinking of his son, Jason, in that potato sack race at the church picnic.

One afternoon while Dale and DJ were fishing in the lake, they heard the dinner bell ringing. Dale, looking at his watch, said to DJ, "It's too early for supper, so whatever Mom wants, it must be important. Let's go back to the house." They picked up their bait bucket and fishing poles and trudged back to the house.

"What's up?" Dale asked as he walked into the kitchen.

"You had a call from some guy, Kevin Langford, who said he needs to speak to you, that it's urgent."

"Kevin Langford? I've never met nor do I know a Kevin Langford."

"This is his phone number," she said handing him a piece of paper. "The area code is 719. I have no idea where that is."

"Well, it must be important. I'd better find out what's so urgent," Dale said as he dialed the number.

"Hello Mr. Langford, this is Dale Karsten, I'm returning your call."

"Yes, thanks for getting back to me. I'm from Colorado Springs, you may have read some of my articles in *The World Today* magazine."

"I do remember the name, now that you mention it. How can I help you, Mr. Langford?"

"Well first off, you can begin by calling me Kevin. I've never been much on formalities. Let me give you a little background. I'm writing a feature article about twins separated at birth. Ironically a good friend of mine here in Colorado fits that category. He's asked me to help find his twin brother. It was only recently that he discovered he was adopted and had a twin brother in Ohio.

"My friend was searching for his college year-book in the attic of his parents' home, when he accidentally knocked over an old box of files. As he began replacing the files, he got the shock of his life while reading the document from an orphanage called Kinder Kare. Long story short, my friend discovered that his birth name was not Rawlins, but. . . "

"Stop, let me guess," Dale interrupted, "his last name was Simmons."

"You got it Dale, Simmons. His twin brother's name is James. On a recent trip to Ohio, I uncovered some of their very tragic story. Their mother is a ward of the state, living a near veg-etative life, if you can call it living. I attempted to interview the administrator, a Dr. Graves, who turned out to be a bit of a pompous ass. However, I did meet a lady who was very help-ful. As a matter of fact, that is where I got your name."

"Anna Frances, am I right?" Dale asked, "How is Anna?"

"Anna's fine, she had a lot of complementary things to say about you, as did other members of the staff. It seems that everybody I inter-viewed recommended that I contact you. I'll be back in your part of the country in a couple of weeks, could we possibly get together? I would love to get your input before putting the story to bed."

"You know, Kevin, it's taken me at least five years and a few counseling sessions to reconcile Jimmy's story in my mind. Your call has brought it all back to me, but I think I can deal with it now."

"I'm sorry to have dredged up any unpleasant past experiences, but I believe you still may have an opportunity to affect his life in a positive way. When I'm in the Cleveland area, I usually stay at a Marriott, but if it's more convenient, I can drive to where you are. I understand it's less than a three-hour drive."

Dale hesitated momentarily as he leafed through a day planner near the phone. "The timing seems okay, and I'd really like to visit some old friends back there, but first, I need to discuss it with my wife."

"Whatever you choose will work for me. I'm looking forward to our meeting."

Dale hung up the phone, looked at Susan and said, "No more rumination. I know how to handle it."

"Yes, you do," she said, smiling up at him. "I heard the whole conversation, and if you need a few days to see it through, we can take care of things. Besides, D.J. is a big help around here now. He's going to feel special being the man of the house."

* * *

It was early afternoon and the Marriott parking lot was almost deserted. Dale walked into the bar that was virtually empty. He was ten minutes early so he bought a beer and found a table with a view of the door. Soon a well-dressed man walked in. He appeared to be around twenty-five years old with curly dark hair. As he approached, Dale stood and shook his hand. "You must be Kevin Langford."

"Guilty as charged, and you must be the infamous Dale Karsten."

Kevin was slightly over six feet tall with a slender build. Dale sat back down when a quick thought came to him that Kevin reminded him of somebody he knew. It wasn't the way he walked in, but a mental flash caused Dale to think that he'd seen that face before. He couldn't figure out who it was, so he let the thought pass. A waitress approached their table as Kevin was unpacking a small tape recorder and a notepad.

"What can I get you gentlemen?" she asked with a friendly smile.

"I'm just nursing this beer," Dale replied. "How about you Kevin?"

"I think I'd like a scotch on the rocks with a little splash of water, Chivas if you have it please." As the waitress walked away, Kevin said, "Do you mind if I get our conversation on tape?"

"Not at all. Tell me, how's your story coming along?"

"It's been quite an experience. I've never visited a psychiatric hospital. I found it extremely fascinating. I must say that Dr. Graves is a piece of work. At first, he seemed very suspicious and defensive, claiming that most journalists are more interested in a good story than the truth. I assured him that his reputation as a highly respected professional would only be enhanced in my story."

"That must've hooked him," Dale said, laughing out loud. "Image is everything to him. I can still see that large collection of very expensive Meerschaum pipes on his credenza, none of which probably ever held tobacco. In my opinion, they were props. I can still see him using his pipe as a pointer in one of his boring lectures, or how he would look down as if meditating, holding his pipe close to his chest pretending to be deep in thought. I believe it was his version of *The Thinker* by the great French artist Auguste Rodin."

Kevin said, "You have him pretty well figured out, Dale! He did that whole pipe routine while I was visiting him in his office, which was very impressive. Once he got the idea that my article might further enhance his reputation, Dr. Graves was extremely cooperative, until the subject of Rachel Simmons being sexually violated was mentioned."

"He again appeared to be defensive, rambling on about how he had conducted a most thorough internal investigation. He explained how he interviewed every employee who was on duty that night and thus came to the only logical conclusion. He assumed that a male patient had removed the heavy protective screen that covered her window. He explained how he learned from the maintenance man that the cage like screen had been pulled back."

"When I asked him for the name of the maintenance person, he again seemed irritated that I might doubt him. He informed me that the man had been long retired, and maybe even deceased. According to Dr. Graves, he did everything humanly possible to solve the unfortunate mystery."

"When I asked him if state or local law enforcement intervened, he informed me that in his professional opinion, it was not necessary. He gave me a list of people on staff who might be helpful. This included Anna Frances, who has a great deal of respect for you. He also listed a gentleman by the name of Peter Fetzer."

Dale appeared to be reading every word on his Budweiser label, but actually, was deep in thought. Finally, he looked up, saying, "Something doesn't add up here. I was told by a reliable source that the maintenance man was roughly 32 to 33 years old, far too young to retire on a janitor's salary."

"Would you mind sharing the name of that source?"

"No. I'm sure Pete would be okay with it."

"Pete, that would be Mr. Fetzer, am I correct? The thing is, I spent a good deal of time with Pete and he never mentioned that he knew the maintenance man that was on that night."

"Depending upon the context of your conversation, it may not have been relevant at the time."

"You could be correct Dale, as I look back, the lion's share of our conversation concerned Jimmy Simmons. It looks like I've missed a few pertinent facts. I'm not back to square one, but I have some more work to do.

"There's one other thing that puzzles me, considering the several people who suggested I speak with you. When your name came up, Dr. Graves gave me an annoyed look, waived his pipe back and forth in a dismissive manner, saying, 'Don't waste your time with that guy.'"

"That doesn't surprise me in the least. I guess you might say that I was a thorn in his side and he saw me as a major irritation. I'm sure you've noticed that Dr. Graves does not like being questioned."

"Well, I believe everybody sees Graves as an insufferable bore and a narcissist, but never mind him for now."

Kevin got the bartender's attention, held up his glass along with Dale's empty bottle, indicating another round. Turning back, he said, "You know, Dale, writing this article about twins separated at birth has become one of the most fascinating and rewarding stories of my career as a journalist. Plus, due to my relationship with Jimmy's brother, this particular segment of the story has become very personal.

"I've interviewed several people who have been most helpful, however, I've found one common denominator. The conversation invariably comes back to you. I expect this place is gonna start filling up in a couple hours, so before the crowd arrives, I would like to hear in your own words, Jimmy's story as you know it."

He waited for the bartender to leave before removing a small handheld tape recorder from his briefcase and laid it on the table in front of Dale. Leaning back with his arms folded across his chest he said, "Anytime you're ready."

Dale sat for a few seconds looking at the ceiling, then down at his lap attempting to get his thoughts together and wondering where to begin.

"As you know, I was simply a psych aid and not a physician by any stretch of the imagination. However, I have always had a keen insight as to people's feelings, especially when they were hurting. This is only my opinion, but I believe Jimmy's problem is similar to what is referred to as a self-fulfilling prophecy, but slightly different."

"Different, how so?" Kevin asked while leaning forward taking a sip of his drink.

"This is how I understand it. When someone seriously believes something about themselves, it invariably comes to pass. If someone sees himself as stupid or a failure, you can bet that prophecy will definitely be fulfilled."

"I understand self-fulfilling prophecy, but how is Jimmy different?"

"In Jimmy's case, I don't believe the prophecy came from within, but from most of the people that he came in contact with from birth. While in the orphanage, people didn't see the normal little kid who only needed love and nurturing, but rather they saw him as one who was born in a mental institution. To add insult to injury, is the product of rape by God knows who. He had been for the most part avoided by everybody and grew up isolated from the real world.

"From the day I met Jimmy, I had a gut feeling that he was a normal kid that just needed some human interaction. Looking back to the first day I met him, he was deathly afraid of water; but within a couple of weeks, I had him jumping into the deep end of the pool. He not only lost his fear of drowning, but the pool became his favorite place.

"On that Thanksgiving when I took him out for the day, I was stunned as to how isolated and unaware he actually was. I still remember him pointing at a phone booth and asking me what it was. I took him to a petting zoo. He had never seen most of the animals. I watched his eyes light up when he fed a small goat out of his hand. While at the park, we stopped at an outdoor café and enjoyed some ice cream. He didn't know the difference between a banana split and a hot fudge sundae. Imagine this, Kevin. He was eleven years old at the time.

"While working at Shady Hills, I spent countless hours reading exit reports from various foster homes, of which one was and still is very troubling. It has not been proven, but there is speculation, along with circumstantial evidence, that he was sexually molested. At another foster home he was traumatized to the point where he was in a catatonic state for two weeks after returning to the orphanage. As the story goes, a couple of older boys crept up behind him one evening and wrapped a large rat snake around his neck. They saw it as a harmless prank, but Jimmy had nightmares for weeks. To make matters worse, a German Shepherd that he had become attached to was hit by a car and died in his arms. I can't imagine anyone going through what Jimmy had to endure and come out of it emotionally unscathed.

"Imagine seeing the other children getting visits, gifts and hugs from visiting relatives, or watching every other kid in your pod going somewhere for the weekend, then eventually being released, while he was always the one left behind.

"I've done extensive research on his background. It's hard to imagine so many tragedies could possibly occur in one family. His great grandmother was abducted years ago and never found. His mother was involved in a head-on collision, where she lost both grandparents. They were her only remaining relatives. Having no family, she became a ward of the state and sent to Pittsfield State Hospital, where she lives today."

All Kevin could do while listening to the living nightmare was to shake his head in disbelief. "You know Dale, not a single person that I've interviewed believes that Jimmy should be in a place like Bainbridge. So, tomorrow morning I'm going to visit that infamous hell hole called a psychiatric hospital."

"You're going there tomorrow? How did you pull that off?"

"I schmoozed my way with Dr. Graves, who

made an appointment for my visit. I had him thinking that he would be the hero in my article. One more thing, Dale. I want you to go with me."

"Whoa, you caught me off guard with that one. I'll call Susan tonight and if everything's going well at home, I'd love to join you. But I don't know how Jimmy will react to a visit from me, or if he'd even recognize me. It's been twelve years. He must be about twenty-four years old now."

"I've taken the liberty of making a reservation for you tonight. We'll discuss our plans over dinner. And don't worry about the cost, I'm on a pretty lucrative expense account."

That evening after dinner Dale called Susan and filled her in on his plans for tomorrow.

"Are you sure you are up to this emotionally, Dale?" she asked.

"I'm fine, those counseling sessions have paid off. I'm looking forward to seeing Jimmy, so don't worry. I'll keep my emotions under control. In the meantime, hug the kids for me and tell them that daddy loves them and daddy loves mommy too."

"We love you too and will say a prayer for you tonight. You know, if Jimmy would have had a family like ours, there's no telling where he'd be today."

CHAPTER THIRTEEN

The following morning, after a quick break-fast at the Marriott, they left for the two-hour, twenty-five-minute drive to Bainbridge Psychi-atric Hospital. As they drove, Kevin turned to Dale, saying, "Tell me what you know about Bainbridge."

"Well, I've certainly heard a lot of stories . . . some are truth and some are legend, I'm still trying to separate the two in my mind."

"Okay, do the best you can and hopefully together we can sort it out."

"I met a guy who worked at this facility and was transferred to Shady Hills. He told me that if he hadn't transferred out of there, he would have switched to another line of work. When I look back at our conversation, I still get chills up my spine.

"From what I've read, the facility was built in the early 1900s. It was called the Bainbridge Lunatic Asylum, then changed to the Bainbridge State Hospital for the Criminally Insane, which is what it's called today. It was a foregone conclusion that once admitted, patients rarely came out alive. This is evidenced by a cemetery along the road leading to the hospital. It's the final resting place for over 500 lost souls.

"Bainbridge had been the home of some of the most notorious criminals in the history of Ohio. You may have read about the famous Oliver Giles, who had an encounter with the angel of Satan. He claims that the angel told him to eat the heart and liver of human beings, which would assure him of eternal life. Over the next few years there were several incidents of missing people in the area. The local police had run out of clues until early one morning at about dawn, a paperboy, while cutting through a backyard, spied a man throwing what appeared to be a young child into a hole in the ground, and covering it up. That day the local police department unearthed more than a dozen graves containing the skeletal remains of his victims.'"

"That is about as sick as it gets," Kevin said shaking his head in disbelief.

"Oh, there's more. Have you ever read the story of a person known as the Lizzie Borden of Ohio?"

"No, I'm afraid I missed that one."

"This woman's name was Abigail Albright, the youngest of a very wealthy family, who torched her home while everyone was sleeping. By the time the fire department arrived, the house was totally engulfed in flames. Young Abigail told the officials that she was trapped in the smoke-filled home, but was finally able to escape with her life. The only flaw in her story was discovered as her clothing showed no signs of smoke, which would not have been possible. After a short interrogation, she confessed to the crimes of murder and arson. Her motive was to be the sole recipient of the family estate, worth over $600 million. The jury took less than two hours to declare her not guilty by reason of insanity. Like the case of Oliver Giles, Abigail was sentenced to life at the Bainbridge Lunatic Asylum. Ironically, they both died within a year of each other and are buried in the hospital cemetery."

"Incredible," Kevin said, pounding on the steering wheel with the palms of his hands.

"This is the stuff that fictional movies are made of. I just can't believe it."

"It gets crazier," Dale remarked matter-of-factly. "Do you remember the attendant I mentioned earlier who transferred from Bainbridge to Shady Hills?"

"Yes, I remember you mentioning a former attendant."

"His name was Doug Garrett. He was a relatively normal and friendly guy, actually very interesting, until he looked at me with a straight face one day at lunch and declared there are ghosts in that place. Not one to believe in ghosts, my expression seemed to have offended him. I apologized for my reaction, telling him that he actually surprised me with his ghost comment. He accepted my apology and went on with his story.

"Doug Garrett declared that he wasn't the only one who had seen the ghosts of Abigail Albright and Oliver Giles walking among the gravestones at night. One evening a female attendant named Karen Kelse had stood with him looking out the third-story window at the cemetery. Suddenly they saw two people holding hands, smiling up at them. According to Doug they pulled the shades quickly, walked away, not wanting to think about what they saw or speak of it. He claimed that after a week or so, he looked up their pictures in the archives, which showed they were indeed the two people he saw that night. They discussed the situation and decided to tell their story. They offered to take a polygraph test, but the doctors explained that a polygraph would not be effective since they both truly believed that what they saw was real. He told me I didn't have to believe him, but he'd go to his grave knowing that what they saw was real."

"Wow, Dale, after hearing your account of the atrocities in that place, my friend back in Colorado will take some serious action. Gerald's family has connections in high places, so I expect he will call in a few favors when he gets my report. It looks like we're about an hour out, so tell me what you know about Kyle Phillips, the current administrator."

"I haven't heard much about him except he can be a real hard ass. He got his start at Pittsfield Hospital before being transferred to Bainbridge. We'll just have to see when we get there. By the way, how do you think he'll accept your bringing me with you?"

Reaching into his jacket pocket and waving

a document, Kevin said, "This is signed by Dr. Graves. Kyle may be a hard ass, but he will not question the good doctor, you can count on it."

Soon they approached a sign that read Bainbridge Hospital, one-quarter mile on the left. They signed in with the guard at the main gate before continuing down the tree-lined road as they passed the cemetery surrounded by a chain-link fence. The grounds appeared to be unkempt and many of the gravestones lay flat on the ground.

"I've always been fascinated by old cemeteries," Dale said. "I wonder if they would allow us to walk through."

"Maybe another time," Kevin said, "but I have a lot of ground to cover with Mr. Kyle Phillips. After hearing the history of this place, perhaps his title should be Warden."

They pulled into a parking lot and walked down a cobblestone sidewalk to the visitor's entrance. Looking around, they observed a cluster of large four-story buildings surrounded by a twelve-foot chain-link fence topped off with concertina wire. There were guard towers every fifty yards surrounding the complex. Everyone entering the complex had to pass through metal detectors before proceeding through an underground tunnel to the main reception area.

After signing several documents and answering countless questions concerning the relationship with the patient, they were led to a sitting room where an elderly woman peered over her reading glasses saying, "Have a seat, Mr. Phillips will be with you shortly." Her personality seemed as drab as her surroundings. The waiting room was lined with chairs in front of a long counter, behind which she sat reading a popular harlequin novel. The walls were green and adorned with black-and-white photographs of downtown Bainbridge fifty years prior, along with the faded, blue drapes. The place indicated that interior decorating was not a high priority.

Looking up, Dale noticed video cameras suspended from the ceiling and suspected that their conversation could be recorded. When the door opened, Dale and Kevin saw a man who literally filled the doorway. He appeared to be about six foot four, weighing roughly two hundred and fifty pounds with very muscular arms and broad shoulders. He looked more like a professional wrestler than a hospital administrator. He had dark curly hair and a goatee which gave him a diabolical look.

With no smile or the offer of a handshake, he waved them into his office saying "I hope this isn't going to take too long as I have a full schedule today."

"We thank you for your time, sir and will make this as brief as possible," Kevin said.

"And what's with the we," he interrupted. "I was told by Dr. Graves that a Mr. Kevin Langford was going to conduct a short interview. Who is your friend here?"

"I'm sorry, but I told Dr. Graves that an assistant would be accompanying me as we are collaborating on the story. I'm sure he forgot to mention it. If you have a problem with it, my assistant would be happy to wait outside."

"No, that won't be necessary. Whatever you want, let's get on with it. As I've said, I have a full calendar."

"I'm sure the doctor informed you that I'm writing an article for The World Today magazine featuring twins who've been separated at birth."

"What would that have to do with Bainbridge State Hospital, may I ask?"

"Well sir, one of the patients in this facility is a twin separated at birth, and he will be one of the persons featured in my article. His name is James R Simmons."

"Yeah, I know all about that. It's a good thing that he is a twin, because the guy is too much of a pain in the ass for one person," he said, chuckling at his own bad joke.

"In what way, sir, do you see him as you say, a pain in the ass?"

"For one thing, he's constantly requesting reading material, as if it would do him any good in this place."

"Reading material?" Kevin asked. What kind of reading material?"

"Everything from law books to books on American history. We had a bleeding-heart social worker visit him one day and he passed her a letter outlining how his constitutional rights were being denied, which got my ass called on the carpet. It seems that every time he's escorted to the infirmary, he draws catcalls from the violent nut jobs on the floor propositioning him for sexual favors."

"It seems to me that your problems are caused by those you refer to as nut jobs."

"Maybe, but the fact remains, since he's arrived, there has been nothing but chaos, and Mr. Simmons is the catalyst. Truth be known, this place would operate much smoother if Mr. Simmons were to be transferred elsewhere.

Now is there anything more I can do for you? If not, I would like to adjourn this meeting."

"Only one more question, sir. What do you know about the sexual attack on Mr. Simmons' mother, and do you believe that all aspects of the case were properly investigated? I ask you this because I know you were an intern at Pittsfield during the time the incident occurred."

Looking at Dale and Kevin with an angry sneer, he stood up, pointing his finger at both men saying, "I don't know what the hell your game is, but that question has absolutely nothing to do with a story about twins separated at birth. Furthermore, I resent you're implying that the investigation could be unprofessional, or I may have had something to do with it." Without saying another word, he walked to the door, opened it and waved his hand in a *you first gesture*, signifying the meeting was over.

"I understand," Kevin said as he retrieved a document from his jacket pocket and unfolded it. "This document says that we are entitled to a thirty-minute private interview with Mr. Simmons." Holding the paper out for the administrator to see he said, "Sir, I apologize if I appeared to be out of line in my questioning, it certainly wasn't intentional."

"Yes, I'm aware of the thirty-minute interview, but I've wasted enough time already. Wait out here. I'll have the chaplain escort you." With that, he turned and walked away with not as much as a goodbye or handshake.

After a short wait, they heard the door open and turned to see a man of small stature, very animated, walking with a quick gait toward them. "Hi, I'm Mike Troutman, the Senior Chaplain." He gave them both a double-handed handshake as he bowed at the waist. I've been instructed to escort you gentlemen to meet with Mr. Simmons. I was told the meeting was not to exceed thirty minutes. Mr. Phillips was most emphatic about the time."

"Before we see Mr. Simmons, would you mind stopping at my office for a few moments where we can speak in private? It's on the way. I assure you it won't cut into your thirty minutes. It's important I get this off my chest."

"Not at all, Dale and I have the rest of the day. We'll be driving back to Cleveland this afternoon."

The chaplain's office wasn't much bigger than a closet with barely enough room for a desk and three folding chairs. As soon as they were seated, the Chaplain began.

"Gentlemen, just between us, for the life of me, I do not understand why Mr. Simmons was committed to this place. Unlike the other patients, he has all of his faculties. Let me explain for you what happened when Mr. Simmons was transferred here. He fell into a depression so deep, he contemplated suicide. He confided to me that he was now in a dark bottomless pit with no way out. His future had become totally hopeless. He was desperate, broken inside, willing to grasp whatever might offer him the slightest hope."

"As Chaplain, it was my duty to attempt lifting him from that pit. One morning he was sitting on his bunk when I tapped on his door. He motioned for me to enter. I asked him the same question I ask everybody. "Do you believe in a higher power? Where are you, spiritually?" The question appeared to irritate him, as he said something like, "They are all hypocrites, just like John Barnes." I didn't know who this Barnes fellow was, so I let the comment go unanswered. Instead, I explained to him that here are hypocrites everywhere; in business, schools and yes, even in churches.

"He sat there mulling over what I had said and nodded in agreement. This was a positive step forward. I gave him a Bible, which he reluctantly accepted. I jotted down two scriptures on a piece of paper and asked him to read them. We agreed we would discuss it on my next visit. This continued for some time. At one point during out times together, he caught me by surprise when he began to quote scripture he had discovered on his own. I began to see a glorious transformation in this young man.

"Before long, he became a prolific reader, not only the Bible, but any reading material he could get his hands on. In all my years as Senior Chaplain, I've never encountered anyone with a more superior intellect, and I certainly never, ever, expected to meet that person here! I've never encountered such a miscarriage of justice. To my knowledge, Mr. Simmons has never had an outside visitor, except for a one-time visit from a volunteer social worker. When I heard you were coming, I wanted to make my feelings known. It's going to take somebody on the outside to right this terrible wrong.

"He's not a violent person. He's soft-spoken and polite. The only thing I ever found on his permanent record was an altercation with a patient who had a reputation for pushing people to the limit. Gentlemen, we all have our breaking point, and I'm sure there's more to the story than what has been recorded."

Dale, throwing both hands in the air, in a victorious gesture, broke into a wide smile and said, "Chaplain Troutman, you have no idea how thrilled I am to hear everything you have just said. I've always believed that about Jimmy's situation, and truly believed he was a product of unfortunate circumstances."

"You can be sure," Kevin interjected, "your words have not fallen on deaf ears. Mr. Simmons case is not over by any means. We are working on a strategy to get him out of here." Handing him a business card Kevin said, "Feel free to contact me at any time and I promise you it will be confidential. Now, if you don't mind, we'd like to visit him."

"Certainly gentlemen," he said, "right this way." They walked down the hall toward Jimmy's room with incredible anticipation, but at the same time not knowing what to expect.

Patient rooms lined the hall on both sides. There were no bars but a glass window to observe patients from the outside and an opening called the food trap where their meals were passed through. As they walked, several patients yelled obscenities and made obscene gestures. You could feel the anger and desperation in the air.

Before Chaplain Mike could unlock the door, Dale looked through the glass, seeing a person lying on his bunk with his feet crossed and a book hiding his face. As the key turned, Jimmy swung his legs off the bed, sat up and laid the book aside. All Dale could think at that moment was, it's him, he's older, but it is definitely him!

He rose slowly from his bunk with a confused expression on his face, never having had an outside visitor, much less two. Suddenly his eyes locked on Dale and his jaw dropped in disbelief. "It's you. Dale, is it really you?" He stood beside his bed not moving a muscle and slowly a smile appeared.

"Yes, it is me, Jimmy, and you don't know how great it is to see you after all these years!" Motioning toward Kevin, Dale said, "This is my friend, Kevin, and you know the Chaplain." Dale took one step toward him extending his hand. Jimmy seemed to stiffen slightly at the handshake so Dale decided to forego a hug, reasoning it would take a while. However, the smile on his face said it all.

"Excuse me gentlemen," said Chaplain Mike, "I'm going to bring in a couple of chairs then

I'll be back in about one-half hour." The Chaplain arrived with two folding chairs and placed them in front of Jimmy as he sat on his bunk. The Chaplain then locked the door and walked away.

Dale sat looking at him, not knowing where to begin. "Jimmy, I keep looking at you and find myself at a loss for words. The last time I saw you, you were only twelve years old."

"It has been a long time, Dale, and I can still remember that great Thanksgiving Day. It was the best day I ever had; the petting zoo, that swinging bridge over the river and my first and only hot fudge sundae.

"I can still taste the food we had that day. Your family was so nice to me and made me feel special. Also, there's another thing that's been bothering me for long time."

"What's that?"

"The day I got angry at you and said I hated you. I didn't hate you; it was just so heart breaking, I didn't know what to say or do. But I want you to know how sorry I am for the way I acted that day. I also want you to know that you were the best friend I ever had; in fact, you are my only friend. These days I find it hard to trust people. It's easier to stay by myself."

Dale interjected, "I totally understand. You have nothing to apologize for. Hopefully, one day soon, we can get together and catch up, but we've only been allowed thirty minutes and my friend Kevin has learned some facts he wants to discuss with you."

Kevin, turning his chair backwards, straddling the chair with his arms leaning on the back, said, "Jimmy, how much do you know about your family?"

"I've heard rumors that I was born in Pittsfield Mental Hospital and that I also might have a twin brother. One time, I overheard some of the staff at Shady Hills discussing my family background."

"You heard correctly. You do have a twin brother; his name is Gerald. He lives in Colorado and is a personal friend of mine. He's asked me to investigate your case and find out where you are. I'm a writer. I investigate and write stories for national magazines. Currently, I'm writing an article on twins separated at birth, and that's where you come in.

"Your brother was adopted by a couple named Chad and Becky Rawlins. Gerald graduated from the University of Colorado and lives in Colorado Springs, near his adoptive parents.

While searching in the attic of their home for his college yearbook, he accidentally knocked over a box containing various files. While picking them up, he discovered a document from an adoption agency called Kinder-Kare, near Akron, Ohio.

"At that point he realized that not only was he adopted, but had a twin brother named James, James Simmons. Gerald was very upset with his parents for keeping his adoption secret. After some days, they talked it out and here's the good news. Mr. Rawlins has agreed to use his political and legal contacts to reunite you with your brother. I know Gerald will be ecstatic when he hears that you are doing so well, both intellectually and emotionally. I don't know how long the process will take; but Jimmy, I can promise you, there's a light at the end of the tunnel. You just need to be patient and keep the faith."

Jimmy answered, "Oh, you don't have to tell me about faith, Kevin. Chaplain Mike and I have had some lengthy spiritual conversations. He has been my anchor in this sea of desperation. Faith has changed my life."

The rattle of the key in the door told them their time was up. As they said their goodbyes, Dale noticed that Jimmy's handshake was different, it was warm and sincere. He also noticed a tear rolling down his cheek.

* * *

They left Bainbridge on State Road 30 toward Interstate 71. Dale was the first to speak.

"So, Kevin, I'm interested in hearing your thoughts about the visit. Not only the conversation with Mr. Phillips and the Chaplain, but especially our visit with Jimmy."

"First, I was surprised by Mr. Phillips. Not because of his truculent personality, but how defensive he became when the subject came up regarding the sexual assault on Mrs. Simmons. That in itself has given me reason to believe that he knows more than what he is saying, or he just might be paranoid.

"I've decided to delay my return home for a couple of days to do a little investigating on my own. I'm going to begin with the maintenance man who supposedly retired at the age of thirty-five, according to Dr. Graves"

"Funny you should mention that," Dale said, "I don't want to read too much into it, but I found his attitude concerning the rape to be suspicious at best. What do you expect to get from the maintenance man?"

"I'm not exactly sure, but there's something fishy about that whole situation with the window screen. I just want to speak to him and get some clarification. How about you Dale, would you be heading home in the morning?"

"No, I'm going to drive back tonight. After everything I've seen, I believe now more than ever the importance of a caring, loving family. I wonder how many of those patients back there had parents like I was blessed with. But you know Kevin, something tells me that Jimmy has a chance at the good life if he's surrounded by the right people. From what you've told me about his brother, I have a feeling that things are going to turn out for the best. My wife calls me an eternal optimist. In this situation, I'm right. What's your story Kevin? I imagine you had a pretty normal childhood."

"My childhood was fairly uneventful, not much to tell. Since we're only five minutes from the hotel, the next time we get together I'll tell you all about it. How's that?"

"Sounds good, I'll look forward to it. You can just drop me off at my car. I'm anxious to get on the road and make it home before the kids go to bed. You have my home number and I have the number of the Marriott. Let's keep in touch. It's been great meeting you and I enjoyed our time together."

After a brief hand shake, Dale threw his suit-case in the back seat and headed for interstate 80, touching his horn twice and giving Kevin one last wave.

CHAPTER FOURTEEN

Three hours later, while being greeted by his family with hugs and kisses, his happy reunion was interrupted by the phone.

Dale answered and was surprised to hear Kevin's voice so soon.

"Dale, the shit has hit the proverbial fan. There was a message waiting for me on my hotel phone from Dr. Graves. He was not very happy, to say the least. He wants me to call him first thing in the morning. I wouldn't have bothered you with this tonight, but Graves made a few uncomplimentary remarks about you being there. I wanted to give you a heads up in case he decides to call you. Anyway, I'll give you a call tomorrow after I speak to him. In the meantime, enjoy your family."

Dale hung up the phone and his first thought

was, I don't work there anymore; why would Graves be concerned about me? I'm ancient history. There's more here than meets the eye. I suspect Kevin has opened a can of worms. This could involve more than just helping Jimmy.

* * *

Kevin called Pittsfield Hospital and asked for Dr. Graves. The secretary announced that Kevin Lankford was on the phone. Dr. Graves answered, "Good, put him through. Dr. Graves here."

"Dr. Graves, this is Kevin Lankford, returning your call."

"Is this the Kevin Lankford that has difficulty following simple instructions?" he said in a condescending tone.

"I'm returning your call as directed," Kevin said, suddenly in no mood for Dr. Graves' sarcasm.

"I received a phone call yesterday from Mr. Phillips, who informed me that you made some insinuations regarding how we handled a most unfortunate incident which took place several years ago. Your tactics are most unprofessional and bordering on a defamation lawsuit."

"Another thing, you fraudulently slipped your accomplice, Mr. Dale Karstan, into the facility, who was not named in my written instructions. Helping an unauthorized person to enter a secure state facility is grounds for legal action. I'm sure your employer, The World Today magazine, would not approve of your venturing outside the intended story, which you claim to be based on twins separated at birth"

"Sir, the woman who was sexually assaulted in a facility under your watch became pregnant, had twins. Those twins were separated at birth. If that doesn't fit my story, I don't know what does."

"Mr. Lankford, I am not inclined to waste my time arguing with you. Questioning my investigation has nothing to do with the birth or separation of twins. Now, effective immediately, you are not to visit any facility that is under my supervision. You are no longer welcome here. If I find out you are interfering in any way, you can be sure there will be legal action taken. Do I make myself clear?"

"I hear you loud and clear *Doctor*. I'll adhere to your orders until I speak to my legal counsel. You can be sure this will all be settled in a court of law. Another thing, *Sir*, you are in control at this point. Remember, I am in control of what I write in the article. For example, I intend to let the readers know that you attempted to control not only my research, but also who I spoke with. This, I'm sure, would not bode well for your reputation."

"Mr. Lankford, are you threatening me?"

"I'm certainly not threatening you. You may want to consider the old adage, the pen is mightier than the sword, if you get my drift."

All of a sudden there was a pause on the line. "Now hold on, Mr. Lankford," the doctor replied in a defensive tone, "there's no reason why we can't work out our differences in a civil way without getting the courts involved. I'm sure we can come to an agreement on what you are permitted to discuss with my staff."

"Doctor, I'm an investigative reporter by trade and I will interview who I want, when I want. If I'm not allowed on hospital property, I'll find another way. You can be assured that I will get my story, and get it right."

"Mr. Lankford, let's not be so hasty," Graves said in a tone becoming more cordial.

"Doctor, I have a lot on my plate today, so I'm going to have to end this conversation. Goodbye!" Kevin hung up the phone and could not stop smiling. This may be one of the few times the pompous bastard didn't get the last word.

* * *

Dale had just finished breakfast with his family. He stood, intending to pour another cup of coffee, when the phone rang.

"It's me Kevin," said the voice on the other end. "I just got off the phone with His Highness, Dr. Graves. I wish you could've heard the panic in his voice. I don't think you'll be receiving a call from him anytime soon. By the end of our conversation you would have thought we were best friends. I'm not going to keep you long, but I wanted to fill you in on my call with Graves. One other thing Dale, before I let you go, do you remember hearing the name of that guy who was the maintenance man on duty the night of Rachel's sexual assault?"

"Yes, I recall being told that his name was Harris, Bill Harris. He lived in Akron at the time, probably William Harris in the phone book. If you can't locate him, I suggest you contact Anna Frances. She has a way of keeping up with everybody."

"Good, I have her home phone number, that way I will not be breaking the emperor's rules by calling the hospital. For your information Dale, I've contacted an attorney who is looking into the legality of my being barred from the institution. I'll let you know what happens; but in the meantime, enjoy your family, we'll talk later."

Hanging up the phone, Kevin searched the white pages and soon found William Harris's phone number. There were three, but fortunately he reached him on the first try.

"Hello, is this the Bill Harris who used to work at Pittsfield Psychiatric Hospital?"

"Yes, it is, who's this? That was a long time ago. What can I do for you?"

"My name is Kevin Lankford. I'm a journalist writing a story on twins separated at birth. The twins I'm referring to were born to a woman who was raped at the hospital."

"That would be Simmons," Bill said immediately. "I'm well aware of the case. In fact, it's what led me to resign. I now work in a regular hospital here in town. My duties are about the same without all the stress and chaos. I don't have to deal with an administrator on a permanent power trip."

"Bill, would you be willing to meet me for lunch tomorrow? I'd really like to get your insight on the happenings at Pittsfield Psychiatric Hospital."

"Sure, I'm off tomorrow. What time, and where would you like to meet?"

"How far are you from the Brown Derby Restaurant on Cedar Avenue?"

"Not far at all, but you've got to promise not to get me involved in something that could affect me or my family."

"You have my word on it; your name will never come up, unless, of course, you choose to testify at some point. Let's meet around eleven thirty so we can beat the crowd. I'll be sitting in the lounge wearing a Cleveland Indians' baseball cap."

It was exactly eleven thirty when Kevin saw a man roughly fifty-five years of age walking towards him. "I see you're also an Indians fan," he said with a broad smile, "I've been suffering with those guys since I played Little League."

"I'm from Colorado myself, and don't know much about the game. I'm staying at the Marriott Cleveland Airport. Whoever was there before me, left his hat behind. I figured it would be a good way for you to recognize me."

The waiter led them to a table in the back and handed them each a menu.

"What would you like to drink?" the waiter asked.

"I think I'll start with water and have coffee later; but I'd like lemon with the water please," Kevin said.

"Water with lemon sounds good; I'll have the same." Bill waited for the waiter to leave and said, "So, how can I help you with your story?"

"Let's get our order in first," Kevin said, while slowly scanning the menu. "Tell me, what's their specialty here?"

"I don't know about a specialty, but I've never had a bad meal in this place. I've always been a meat and potatoes guy, so I'm going for the half-pound burger with fries."

When the waiter arrived to take their order, Kevin said, "Whatever my friend has, I'll have the same, without the fries." He twisted a lemon wedge into his water.

After the waiter removed their plates, Kevin produced his ever-present tape recorder and laid it on the table. While slowly stirring his coffee, he said, "You mentioned on the phone yesterday that you resigned from Pittsfield. You felt that Kyle Phillips, along with the administrator, Dr. Graves, had something to do with your resignation. Could you elaborate on that?"

"Sure, I'd be glad to. You know, I may be oversensitive, but I didn't like the way they threw their weight around. Everything was a direct order. Harris, do this, Harris do that. Never please or a thank you, always calling me by my last name like I was some kind of peon. But the straw that broke the camel's back was when Graves ordered me not to speak to anybody regarding the window screen on Mrs. Simmons room. I mentioned that the screen was not pulled out far enough for an adult to climb through, and he told me that I needed to stick with being a janitor and leave the thinking up to him. I wanted to kick the shit out of him right there. So, as soon as I found another job, I left."

"After that, I pulled some strings and actually recommended my cousin Alex, who now has my old job. He's the quiet type, unlike me, he does his job and doesn't get involved in the day-to-day crap that goes on there. I never had a good feeling about those two people."

"Besides Phillips and Graves, did you have a problem with anybody else on the staff?"

"No, for the most part everybody was pretty easy to get along with. Actually, I didn't have a great deal of contact with Graves, except for that incident regarding the window screen. Kyle Phillips was a real jerk. I never did like that asshole, or trust him. Most of the women he worked with couldn't stand him. They referred to him as Creepy Kyle."

"That's not the most complimentary nick-name," Kevin said, chuckling. "Wow did he acquire that handle?"

"The ladies often complained that he would leer at them with a creepy look on his face. Make inappropriate remarks. A few of the women went to Graves and complained; but nothing was done about it. In fact, those who reported him eventually quit, as they were suddenly assigned the worst possible duties. Phillip's favorite saying was, "When you screw with me, paybacks are hell."

"It was common knowledge that if you wanted to keep your job you didn't cross Creepy Kyle. The only person he never clashed with was the big man himself."

"I assume you are referring to the adminis-trator, Graves, correct?"

"Yeah, Graves, but they're birds of a feather, those two. When the position of Administra-tor opened up at Bainbridge State, it was no surprise when creepy Kyle got the job. The standard joke among the staff was that his promotion gave a whole new meaning to the old adage, *the inmates are running the asylum.*"

Kevin handed the waiter his American Express card before turning to Bill. "I appreciate you meeting with me today. I'll be in town a few more days at the Cleveland Marriott. If you think of anything that could be pertinent to my article, you can reach me there." Handing him a business card, he added, "This is my home office in Colorado Springs, but I check for messages several times a day."

While pulling out of the restaurant parking lot, Kevin noticed the gas gauge was on empty. After filling up at a Sunoco station, he headed down Route 21 to Cleveland, planning to work on his article.

Just as he was opening the door to his room, he heard the phone ring inside. It was the attorney.

"Kevin, this is Steve Abrams. I want to give you an update on my conversation with Dr. Graves. By the way, you had me thinking he was some kind of an ogre, but he couldn't have been more pleasant and cooperative."

"I'm not surprised Steve. Perhaps he thought I was bluffing when I told him that I was prepared to take legal action. My father always said, if you want to make a bully stand down, ya gotta stand up to him."

"Your dad sounds like a wise man. Let me get right to the point, Kevin. I read all the legal statutes, chapter and verse, to Graves regarding entering public facilities. The only way to prohibit anybody from visiting the hospital is if they are disruptive, and of course carrying a firearm or any illegal activity such as drugs. He understands that you are entitled to enter the building or any facility and speak to anybody only if they are on break or during lunch. Otherwise you're free to interview anybody off the premises."

"Does that mean I can visit patients?"

"Yes, I made that clear to Dr. Graves, at which time he made a tasteless remark."

"And what was the remark, might I ask?"

"He said if you're planning to visit Mrs. Simmons, you could spend thirty minutes talking to the wall and save the trip. That struck me as very, very unprofessional."

"Well counselor, based on what I've heard, nothing he says would surprise me. But, back to Jimmy, if I may. I spoke to his brother in Colorado and he's determined to free him from

that glorified prison called Bainbridge Psychiatric Hospital, as well as any psychiatric institution for that matter. He indicated that he
may be forced to use his family's political in-
fluence, but is prepared to do what has to be
done. I told him about you and how you handled my situation. He is very impressed. You
will probably be hearing from him soon."

"I appreciate that Kevin, if I can help you in
any way, please don't hesitate to call."

"You've been such a help already by ensuring
my entrance to Pittsfield Hospital. I'm planning to visit Rachel Simmons tomorrow. I don't
know what to expect, but for my friend's sake
and Jimmy's, I'm not going to leave a stone
unturned. Besides, it may enhance my story
for The World Today magazine."

"That makes perfect sense to me, Kevin, and
by the way, how is the story coming?"

"Pretty well, I just need to put all the pieces
together. Since so many of the pieces are here
in Ohio, I've taken a three-month lease on a
small apartment not far from here. With what
it would cost me to fly back and forth, I'm better
off spending my time where the action is."

"Excellent! Let's meet for lunch soon. I'm
anxious to hear about your visit with Rachel."

"I'll keep you posted. I'm certainly looking forward to getting together for lunch sometime soon." Kevin hung up the phone and spent the next half-hour formulating his plan for tomorrow's visit.

* * *

The young attendant led him down a long hallway toward room seven in cottage three. Kevin noticed that everything was painted in a kind of faded green, prompting him to ask the attendant why the colors were not brighter and more cheerful, considering the depressed condition of most patients.

She explained to him that all psychiatric institutions in Ohio use that same color green. It's based on an extensive study by the American Psychiatric Association. This particular color was beneficial to reduce anxiety and bring about a calmer state of mind, since anxiety is the most prevalent psychiatric disorder in the general population.

As Kevin entered the room, he saw a slender woman sitting in a rocking chair with a light blanket over her knees. Her hair was tied in a short ponytail. There was no movement as she appeared to be staring out the window. It was apparent that she was totally oblivious of the beautiful flower garden and two squirrels playing in a tree just outside her window. The first thing that came to his mind was the famous painting, *Arrangement in Grey and Black* by James McNeil, or commonly known as Whistler's Mother. He was surprised that after more than twenty-four years, she was still quite attractive, despite her pallid complexion due to the lack of sunshine.

He pulled up a straight back chair and looked into her empty eyes. Taking one of her hands in his, he began to speak softly. "Hi Rachel, my name's Kevin, it's nice meeting you. I know your family; they think about you often. They live far from here, but know where you are and will come to see you soon."

He was hoping for some kind of reaction, even if it was only eye movement, but there was nothing. For the next half-hour he commented about everything that came to mind, hoping that human interaction would have some effect on her.

"The flowers outside are beautiful," he said smiling, "and the sun is shining brightly, and aren't those squirrels cute?"

Still nothing. After exhausting everything he

could think of to say, he looked at his watch and realized it was time to leave.

"I've got to go now," he said, patting her hand gently. "I'll be back tomorrow and I'll visit you often." He smiled but she didn't respond. As he left the building, he softly said to himself, "My God, nobody deserves what that poor woman is going through, even though she's unaware of the world and everything around her."

Over the next two weeks, Kevin visited Rachel six times with no reaction whatsoever. But today, he got a pleasant surprise. He finally saw a response. A slight response, but a response nonetheless. Every day he would try something different, from playing Frank Sinatra and Perry Como on a small recorder, to actually singing hymns that he learned back in Sunday school. Today he decided to try poetry. He read, *Hope is Anything with Feathers* by Emily Dickinson, and *A Girl's Garden* by Robert Frost. He even read, *The Village Blacksmith* by Longfellow, hoping that something might get a reaction.

Just before leaving, he decided to read one more. When he got to the last line of a poem called, *Trees* by Joyce Kilmer, it happened. "*Poems are made by fools like me but only God can make a tree."* He watched in stunned silence as she slowly raised her right hand from her lap and pointed directly at a large oak tree outside her window. "You heard me!" he exclaimed, unable to control his excitement. "You understood."

He couldn't stop smiling on the way home. He had to call somebody; he had to share the good news. When he got home, he immediately dialed his attorney, hoping to set up that lunch date they had discussed. Steve's secretary put him on hold while she announced Kevin Lankford was on line four.

"Guess who I was just going to call?" came Steve's voice on the other end. "I was wondering if we could meet for lunch tomorrow, I have some very interesting news to share."

"Ditto my friend, I have something to share with you as well. What time and where?"

"How about eleven thirty at the Brandywine Tavern?"

"Brandywine at eleven thirty it is. I'll see you there."

Kevin found a parking spot near the restaurant entrance. Picking up his small tape recorder along with a notepad, he checked his watch, not wanting to be late. While walking in the direction of the entrance, he noticed a yellow Mercedes convertible pull in and park in the far corner of the lot.

It was Steve Abrams who approached him with a wide smile and firm handshake. "It's good to see you again Kevin, have you been here before?"

"Yes, Dale Karsten and I had dinner here once. The food was outstanding, not exactly the place to eat when you're on a diet," he said, patting his stomach. "You parked so far away, I thought I was in the wrong place."

"This place fills up pretty fast. I don't need people opening their car doors into my baby over there," he said, pointing to the yellow Mercedes.

"I know what you mean, I do the same thing with my car, but I'll let Hertz worry about this one."

"Hertz, that must be costing you a fortune. You've already been here a month and you have a short-term lease on an apartment."

"My dad is in the automobile business and well connected with the rental companies. I'm enjoying a professional courtesy."

The waiter led them to a booth in the back and handed them each a menu.

"What can I get you gentlemen to drink?"

"Just water for me," Kevin said, "it's early."

"Hell, it's five o'clock somewhere," Steve said. "I'll have a Chivas on the rocks, with a splash. Like they used to say in law school, image is everything. If you ain't successful, fake it till you make it. Drink Chivas Regal and drive a Mercedes."

"And wear Carrera sunglasses and a Rolex," Kevin said with a wry smile.

"You're very observant for a young man. How old are you anyway?"

"I'll be twenty-five in June."

"I have a son your age, a professional student. I always dreamed of him joining me in my law firm. Abrams and Abrams has a nice ring to it. But, unfortunately, the law profession didn't appeal to him. He got his undergraduate and Master's Degree at Ohio State, majoring in education. He wants to be a teacher, a college professor. As we speak, he's working on his doctorate at Hiram College, not far from here. My dad always said, find a job you love and you'll never work a day in your life, so I should be happy for Steve Junior."

"Sounds a lot like me. My dad wanted me to join him in business management, but my passion is writing. I actually had a short story published when I was a senior in high school."

When the waiter delivered their food, Steve asked, "So what's this exciting news you mentioned on the phone yesterday?"

"Well, thanks to you, I was able to visit Rachel Simmons. I go three times a week, trying everything under the sun, in hopes of breaking through. Something told me from the beginning that she is in there. Somebody had to find a way to communicate with her."

"I spoke to a doctor friend back in Colorado who encouraged me to keep trying. He explained that the most powerful force in our lives is human touch and speech. I did everything from playing music, to singing hymns and reading stories from children's books, with no results. Yesterday, was poetry day. I was just about to give up, but decided to try one more. I read a popular poem by Joyce Kilmer entitled *Trees*. You're not going to believe this, but when I finished the line, *only God can make a tree,* she raised her hand and pointed at the tree outside her window. I know that doesn't sound like much, but to me it was a major victory. Now, more than ever, I am determined to keep on working with her."

"That is exciting, Kevin. I'm honored that you wanted to share that with me. Keep up the good work. I think you may be onto something. Now, I have some news for you. It seems your friend in Colorado is well-connected with people in high places. I got a call from Bainbridge Psychiatric Hospital informing me that Mr. James Simmons is eligible to be released in the care of a person who will sign an affidavit to be responsible for him."

"Seriously, are you telling me we can get him out of that place?"

"That's exactly what I'm saying. They are sending legal forms to my office which must be signed by you and notarized. He will not be allowed to leave the state for a period of time while the state follows his progress. He will have a 10:00 PM curfew.

"Your challenge, if you decide to be his legal guardian, will be to slowly acclimate him to the outside world. You and I cannot imagine what it must be like, adapting to everything we take for granted, like shopping malls, supermarkets and all the rules that govern our behavior in this crazy world. A world he only knew briefly in his foster homes.

"Oh, there's one other thing. I'm sure you've

seen the one size fits all baggy state-issued clothing. He will need a full set of clothing, along with shoes, socks and underwear. You can call a Miss Gina Watkins at the facility. I'm sure she can have someone get his measurements so that you can get standard sizes. The least we can do is make sure that he is dressed for the outside world."

"I totally agree, when can I pick him up?"

"They're going to need a couple days to process the paperwork. Let's see, tomorrow is Saturday, so, I imagine Tuesday would probably work, but I would call ahead and confirm it."

"Tuesday works well for me; it would give me time to shop for the necessary clothing and personal items for Jimmy."

* * *

Kevin walked into J.C. Penney Saturday morning carrying the list of clothing and sizes Gina had provided. He was a bit surprised that he and Jimmy both wore the same size shirts and pants, except his shoes were a half size smaller After purchasing blue jeans, shirts and underwear, he walked next-door to the Thom McCann shoe store. After looking at everything from canvas Keds to wingtips, he settled on a pair of comfortable looking black loafers.

The only thing left was a trip to the drugstore for a razor, shaving cream and deodorant. Fortunately, the two-bedroom apartment he rented was furnished. He looked over his checklist one last time. Everything appeared to be in order. There was nothing left to do except work on his article, and wait with anticipation for Tuesday.

Kevin woke up Tuesday morning at 6 o'clock without need of an alarm clock. His mind was too busy to think about being hungry, so he had half a cinnamon roll and a cup of black coffee. Taking a second cup for the road, he began the hundred and sixty-five-mile trip, south on Interstate 71 to Bainbridge, Ohio. He planned to arrive around 10:30 AM.

With his mind racing in all directions, he decided to find a country music station on the radio. As he turned off Interstate 71 onto State Road 30, he realized that he needed gas. After gassing up at an Esso station, he saw a sign: Bainbridge, 77 miles. Listening to the music had a calming effect. Willie Nelson singing, *Blue Eyes Crying in the Rain*, Eddie Arnold's *Bouquet of Roses* and Patsy Cline singing *I Fall to Pieces* helped pass the time.

Rounding a bend, he noticed a sign, Bainbridge hospital one mile. He turned left onto the hospital property. He remembered that unkempt cemetery on the left and saw the stark grey building with the guard towers. He couldn't help but smile at the irony of Johnny Cash singing *Fulsome Prison Blues*.

Like his last visit, the procedure was the same. First, check in. Fill out and sign a variety of forms. The noxious odor was also the same as he was led through the drab dark tunnel to the waiting area. He asked the receptionist to announce his arrival to Miss Gina Watkins.

Soon, Miss Watkins stepped into the lobby and said, "Hello, Mr. Langford." Unlike Kyle Phillips, she gave him a friendly smile and a warm handshake.

"It's a pleasure to meet you, Mr. Langford," she said. "Mr. Simmons should be joining you within the next thirty minutes. But first, we need to get him presentable. I assume the bag you're holding contains his clothes."

"Yes, they do. I certainly appreciate your gracious cooperation. I'm in no hurry. We've waited a long time for this moment, so, thirty minutes will be just fine."

Kevin sat down in one of the well-worn,

leather chairs in the waiting room. He began to form a mental list of what to talk about on the way home. He assumed that someone who had virtually spent a lifetime in isolation, unfamiliar with the outside world, would present a challenge.

The unpleasant atmosphere caused him to appreciate the world in which he grew up. Not only the surroundings, but the cacophony of sounds was beyond depressing. Desperate cries, angry shouts and patients pounding on the walls while the attendants constantly barked orders. He made a promise to himself, at that moment, to remember this place and count his blessings daily.

Suddenly, his thoughts were interrupted by the sound of footsteps. Looking up, he saw the smiling face of James Ronald Simmons.

"You did it! Mr. Langford. I knew this would happen since the day you and Dale Karsten came to visit me. I don't know how to thank you."

"This is the first day of the rest of your life, Jimmy. I'm happy to be a part of it. And please, call me Kevin. If you have your personal belongings, we can hit the road and never look back."

"I only have two possessions. One is the Bible the Chaplain gave me. As he reached into his pocket, he withdrew a small harmonica. "Several years ago, at Christmas time, when I was at Shady Hills, I got this gift and a card from Dale Karsten. I keep the card in my Bible and look at it often. Since I had all the time in the world to practice, I got pretty good at playing the harmonica!"

"I know Dale is a good friend of yours and you are very important to him as well. I expect you two will see a lot of each other in the future. So, if you're ready, let's go home."

While leaving the hospital parking lot, Kevin turned and asked, "Do you prefer to be called James, Jim, or Jimmy?"

"Dale always called me Jimmy, so I'd like to be called Jimmy from now on."

Attempting to make conversation, Kevin asked, "Did you ever think this day would come?"

"I knew this day would come. I just didn't know when, but I knew it would happen."

"You're a positive thinker. That will take you a long way in the future."

"It's faith, Kevin. If we have the faith of a mustard seed, we can move mountains."

"Wow, that's profound, where did that come from?"

"It came from the Bible."

"So, you're somewhat of a Bible scholar, I take it?"

"Like I said before, I had nothing but time. I didn't want to waste a minute of it. I read everything I could get my hands on ... magazines, Reader's Digest, and the Bible, of course. Someone once said, your mind is like a muscle, if you don't use it, you'll lose it."

"I'm amazed at you," Kevin said, shaking his head in disbelief. "Your wisdom goes far beyond most people I know who have never faced anything close to what you have endured. Tell me, what's your secret? I understand that reading magazines, books and bibles could somewhat keep you abreast of the times. But there must be more. How on earth did you keep your sanity all those years when everyone around you was suffering from some kind of mental illness?"

"Mental illness is misunderstood. I think some of the so-called psychiatrists were as mentally deficient as their patients. After a short session, to justify their position, they felt obligated to make a diagnosis. These doctors are great at putting labels on people: schizophrenic, anxiety disorder, manic-depressive, and clinical depression to name a few. Everybody got a label, but treatment was scarce."

"So how did you manage without treatment?"

"I treated myself based on articles I had read."

"Self-diagnosis and self- treatment? I find that impossible to comprehend."

"Diagnosis was no problem, because I knew I would be okay as long as I didn't fall into a self-defeating mindset. I read an article in Reader's Digest about how prisoners of war maintained their sanity through long periods of isolation. I remember reading about one man who claimed all he needed was an active imagination. He would lay in his cell at night and imagine walking through a beautiful park. There on a park bench, he met an older man who was reading a newspaper. In his mind, he actually struck up a conversation with the man. It's a beautiful day he said, any good news in that paper, or the same old junk?

"He eventually got so good at this technique that he literally heard the sounds of children in the distance and saw swans swimming across a beautiful pond. He had the ability to make it so real that he actually looked forward to their visit the next day. One day they would walk through the park while the old man told stories of his life. He was a widower and most of his friends had passed away. He felt a sense of purpose visiting the man who never failed to show his gratitude with a thanks for coming today and I hope to see you again tomorrow."

"He perfected this imagination technique to the point where often he would forget his current circumstances locked up in a cold dark cell. I'll never forget what one former prisoner said, that being imprisoned and isolated, does not destroy all the people all of the time. Some are resilient, even during the bleakest times, they find opportunities to not only mature, but to flourish.

"That one sentence changed the way I looked at the future. I could give up and just exist, or I could spend my time preparing myself for what actually took place today. I read a quote from an English gentleman named Francis Bacon who said, *knowledge is power.* I came to realize that I was powerless, but nobody could deprive me of knowledge. To me, it all came down to survival."

"You know, Jimmy, I have a confession to make. For the last couple of days, I've been agonizing over how I would keep a conversation going with someone who had been deprived of human interaction for so long. But I've got to tell you, I'm flabbergasted, simply dumbfounded. During the last hour you have been so articulate and interesting. I've hung on your every word. I couldn't have gotten a word in if I wanted to, which I didn't. Let's find a restaurant and have some lunch. I can't wait to continue our conversation."

"That sounds good to me, Kevin. I know you've gone to a lot of expense traveling to visit me and picking me up today. Even the clothes I am wearing. I want you to know that I will pay you back for everything as soon as possible."

Kevin held his palm up in a stop gesture. "Please, don't concern yourself about that. I see big things for you in the future. I'm just happy that I got the opportunity to be a part of it. I could not have paid for all I learned from you concerning human survival. I'm looking forward to our time together. I'm sure you've barely scratched the surface today. Well, look, there's a sign for IHOP, one mile on the right. How's pancakes sound, Jimmy?"

"Sounds good to me. I've never been to an IHOP or any restaurant for that matter, so this will be a new experience."

As they entered the restaurant, a sign read, seat yourself. They chose a booth near the window, which looked out at a field surrounding a lake with a herd of cattle grazing.

"That's a nice view," Jimmy said. "I imagine most people would just take it for granted. I've heard people say, you don't appreciate what you have until it's gone, but with me, I don't know what I've missed, until I see it."

The waitress handed each of them a menu and took their order for coffee. When she returned, Kevin was fascinated as Jimmy politely thanked her and began scanning each page of the menu casually before ordering eggs over light, with bacon and rye toast, as if he'd done it a thousand times.

Kevin sat, slowly stirring his coffee. He was surprised to look over to see Jimmy with his hands folded and his head bowed, saying grace. He was lost for words.

Jimmy looked up, unfolded his napkin and placed it in his lap, then said, "Is something wrong? You seem to have lost your appetite."

"It's not that. I've been watching your impeccable table manners. Where did that come from?"

"It came from movies."

"Movies? You've lost me."

"Occasionally, patients who were not disruptive, they called us trustees, would be taken to the activity room where they would show us movies. I spent my time watching how people on the outside behaved. How they used their silverware and napkins during meals, how they interacted with each other. As a matter fact, I spent so much time studying the people's actions, that I never knew how the story ended. The movies were my school. I had to learn the habits of regular people because I knew one day, I'd be one of them."

"You are one of them, Jimmy. I'm sure there's a lot of things left to experience. You can be sure I'll do everything in my power to get you up to speed. Tell me, have you thought about your immediate plans?"

"The first thing I need to do is to become financially self-reliant, which means I'll have to find employment as soon as possible. I'm hoping to see Dale soon and catch up. I understand he has two children and I know he must be an excellent husband and father."

"I've kept in touch with Dale by phone. He knows you're being released. He indicated that he would like to see you once you're settled in.

Anna Frances and Pete Fetzer also ask about you often and are anxious to see you again. What do you say we get moving, so we'll be home before dark?"

Kevin paid the waitress and instructed her to keep the change. They walked outside and before getting in the car, Jimmy stopped to gaze at the surroundings.

"I've seen pictures similar to this, but the cattle never moved, the trees didn't sway and the air didn't smell this fresh. I've also never felt so free," he said, his voice cracking with emotion.

Side by side, they leaned on the fence watching the cattle graze. Kevin was not about to interrupt the moment.

"You know, Jimmy," he said, while staring straight ahead, "there's a million moments like this just waiting to happen. Every day there will be something new. In a way, I envy you, because I, like most people, have taken my life for granted."

Jimmy nodded. "To me, it's kind of like someone being blind from birth for twenty-five years and one day, their eyes are filled with light. You're right, Kevin, there's a lot to see and do. I can't wait to get started. So, maybe we should move on to my next adventure."

Back on the road they both were silent for the next few miles. Jimmy's head seemed to be on a swivel, not wanting to miss anything. Occasionally he would break into a smile when he saw something as simple as a young boy walking his dog, or a flock of birds flying overhead.

Kevin was the first to break the silence. "I'm curious about something."

"Curious about what?" Jimmy asked, still gazing out the window.

"I was told that your last two years at Shady Hills, you were somewhat of a major challenge, that you were disruptive and combative."

"That might be an understatement. What you heard was one hundred percent correct. But then, I got the biggest and best wake-up call of my life."

"What happened? What caused the drastic turnaround in your life?"

"It wasn't until I got transferred to Bainbridge that things began to change. I met Chaplain Mike. Just like Dale Karsten, he cared and it showed. It wasn't merely a job to him. He listened more than he spoke.

"Unlike many chaplains, who throw a bunch of Scripture at you expecting you to know what it meant, when Chaplain Mike quoted Scripture, he not only explained it but helped me see how it applied to my life. He helped me to deal with some of the attendants who were on a power trip, barking orders and throwing their weight around. He spoke to me often about forgiveness, which I have been working on ever since.

"You see, with Dale gone and Pete Fetzer being assigned to the young kids, I felt deserted. I felt abandoned and I acted out my frustration. Miss Anna was great, but being in charge of the entire hospital, she didn't have time to dedicate to one person. When I reached the age of 16, I was transferred to Pittsfield Psychiatric Hospital for adults. I was still angry there and lashed out verbally at everything and everybody. I got into trouble when a crazy bully kept pushing me around and I lost it. Things went downhill from there and finally they transferred me to Bainbridge.

"When Chaplain Mike came to visit me, he hardly said a word. He sat, listening to me whine and complain how everybody was against me and what a poor victim I was. How I felt I'd never have a normal life and why should I live. Still, Chaplain Mike did not speak, but wrote some words on a notepad and handed it to me. He told me to read it every day until he returned. It wasn't a lot, but it spoke volumes if you took it seriously and meditated on its meaning. After he left, I unfolded the note and he was correct, it was a very short message."

"And what did the note say?" Kevin asked, while leaning on every word.

"It was the motto of the State of Ohio, the state motto."

"Which is?" Kevin asked, looking somewhat confused.

"With God, all things are possible."

"That's it? That's all? I don't mean to trivialize it; he gave you a simple motto from the State of Ohio?"

"It's more than that, Kevin, it comes directly from the Bible, Matthew 19:26. In fact, it's the only state motto in the country that comes from Scripture, verbatim. The next time he came, he gave me a bible as a gift. He wrote two Scriptures on a little piece of paper and asked me to read and meditate on them. Said, he would be back in a few days. One was Philippians 4:13, and the other one was Isaiah 41:10."

"I'll look those up when I get a chance, I really will," Kevin promised.

"You don't have to; I'll recite them for you.

"I can do all things through Christ who strengthens me. Fear not, for I am with you; be not dismayed, for I am your God; I will strengthen you, I will help you, I will uphold you with my righteous right hand."

"Wow, I'm impressed, that came right off the top of your head."

"You may find this hard to believe, but I have memorized the entire Old Testament, and I'm up to the book of Acts in the New Testament. It not only helped me pass the time, but most important of all, it changed my life. I decided, as Chaplain Mike always said, if it is to be, it's up to me."

For a moment, Kevin didn't speak, but slowly shook his head. "Considering where you've been, you've probably never heard this, but you, my friend, are an amazing person.

Tell me, what's the first thing on your agenda? What is your plan beginning tomorrow?"

"The first thing I need to do is find employment. Anything. Chaplain Mike always said the best place to find a helping hand is at the end of your arm."

"Chaplain Mike sounds like my kinda guy. I can understand why you admire him so much.

Good old common sense isn't so common these days.

"As long as we're on the subject of employment, I may have some good news for you. As I was leaving Pittsfield hospital the other day, I ran into Anna Frances. She was summoned to a meeting by Dr. Graves. She was thrilled to hear of your release. She mentioned her brother owns an upscale restaurant called the Garden of Eatin, walking distance from our apartment. It would be menial work to start. Anna promised to speak to him and get back to us. It might be bussing tables, or washing dishes, but a job is a job until something better comes along. Would something like that interest you?"

"I don't care if I have to scrub toilets. It's honest work, and somebody has to do it. I really appreciate your mentioning me to Miss Anna. Next to Dale, she was always one of my favorite people."

"After getting a job, what next?"

"My plan is to study for a high school graduate equivalent degree, then attend a junior college and major in Christian counseling. I can't imagine anybody, no matter how messed up their life is, that I would not be able to relate to and hopefully help them, as Chaplain Mike and Dale did with me. Oh, by the way, what were you doing at Pittsfield the other day?"

"I was doing what you and I are going to do together, if and when you're up to it. I was visiting a lovely lady by the name of Rachel Simmons, your mother."

"Oh my God, you don't know how many times I've dreamed of seeing and speaking to my mother! From what I've been told, she's in a vegetative state and doesn't recognize anybody. But I still want to see her. As a matter of fact, I would like to see her as often as possible. I realize walking into that building will be painful, but at least I'll be allowed to walk out. Tell me, Kevin, what's she like and is she totally unresponsive as I've been told?"

"She has the appearance of an attractive middle-aged woman. If you didn't know the story, you would think she was as normal as anybody, by looking at her. Yes, I know what the doctors say, but my instincts tell me the doctors could be wrong. I believe there is hope for her. I saw something with my own eyes. I believe, with loving human interaction she, like you, will experience a miraculous transformation. Don't ask me how; I just know,

I just know."

Jimmy was silent and seemed to be in deep thought. Looking at Kevin, he said, "Truly I tell you, if you have faith like a grain of mustard seed, you can say to this mountain move from here to there, and it will move, nothing will be impossible for you."

"Is that another Bible verse?" Kevin asked.

"Yes, yes, it is, and I believe it with all my heart."

They continued the drive in a comfortable silence, each lost in their own thoughts.

"There's a welcome sign," Kevin announced, "Northfield 18 miles, we're almost home. But first, we need to stop at a supermarket and pick up some things. That in itself should be a new and interesting experience."

Kevin turned into a shopping mall and parked in front of a store called PICK-N-PAY.

Jimmy stepped out of the car scanning his surroundings, reading out loud, JCPenney, Walgreens pharmacy, ABC liquor, and every other store in the mall.

Kevin stood watching him, thinking, to Jimmy, this must be like visiting a distant planet. Again, he was in no hurry to interrupt the moment.

After visually taking everything in, Jimmy said, "I'm ready, let's go."

The first thing that surprised him was the supermarket door opened by itself. Before he could process the magic door, he stopped cold in his tracks at the view before him. Everything you could imagine; it was all there! People were pushing these big baskets on wheels, taking whatever they wanted. He stood in awe, again reading the signs: bakery, dairy, meat, poultry and deli. It suddenly occurred to him that all the movies he studied at the hospital barely scratched the surface of what the real world had to offer. Realizing that Kevin was probably anxious to get home, he turned and said, "I'm sorry for holding us up, I'll have plenty of time in the future to catch up and work on that transformation we spoke of."

Kevin picked up some bananas and strawberries in the produce section. As they turned up another isle, he picked up a carton of Budweiser, hesitated momentarily, before putting it back on the shelf.

Jimmy was quick to respond saying, "Please, don't put that back because of me. I'm sure you drink responsibly or you wouldn't be where you are today. However, I've seen a lot of people in the hospital who destroyed their lives, and the lives of their family with drugs and alcohol. I made a decision that when I entered society, I would abstain from any substance that may be mind altering. I understand that anybody who partakes responsibly will not have a problem, but personally, I'm not going to take that gamble. So please, don't change your daily routine on my account."

"Thanks, you're absolutely right," Kevin said while putting the beer back into the cart. "The next few months are going to be quite an experience. I suspect both of us will go through a learning process. I can't think of anything else we need, so let's go home."

They arrived at the apartment complex, drove under a wrought iron arch that said Avalon Estates, and maneuvered into their personal carport. Up ahead on the door were the numbers 216. "We're home Jimmy, let's go in and check out your new digs."

Kevin fished a keychain from his jacket pocket, and said while he removed one key, "Here is an extra key to the apartment. You'll need it when I'm not home."

Kevin led the way, unlocked the door while pushing it open, motioning him to go on in.

Jimmy took two steps into the apartment and stopped. Seeing a full kitchen to his left, tables, chairs, a stove and refrigerator brought back memories of the foster homes from years ago.

"So, what do you think?" Kevin questioned, removing a cold beer from the fridge. "Let's see, we've got Coke, milk and orange juice. Would you like something to drink?"

"Nothing right now thanks. Maybe later, but now I'd just like to look around, if that's okay with you."

"Please do, that's your room," Kevin said, pointing toward the door on his left.

"Kevin watched as Jimmy stood opening and closing the door. After doing this several times, Kevin asked, "Is there something wrong with the bedroom door?"

"No, there's nothing wrong with the door, it's just that I'm not accustomed to doors that are unlocked. I know that may sound silly, I'm sure I'll get used to it."

"You have your own private bath and shower, also the dresser and closet for your things. It appears that we both wear the same size clothing, so I put a few pairs of jeans, shirts and socks in your drawer which will get you through for a while. Take your time looking around, I'm going to watch some TV."

Jimmy stood looking at his reflection in the full-length mirror on his bedroom door. You look pretty normal, he thought to himself. While checking out his room, he heard Kevin call, "Jimmy, it's a phone call for you."

Who in the world would be calling me here, or even knows I'm here? As he walked out of his room, Kevin was standing there holding the receiver against his chest, and motioning him forward.

He whispered, "It's Chip Francis, Anna's brother who owns the restaurant we talked about. He wants to speak to you. I'll turn the TV down so you can hear," he said in a whisper, handing Jimmy the phone.

"Hello, this is Jimmy Simmons."

"Hello Jimmy, I'm Chip Francis. My sister, Anna, told me that you're looking for a job. I certainly could use some additional help around here, if you're interested."

"Yes sir, I sure am, when can I come see you?"

"The sooner the better, as far as I'm concerned. How about tomorrow? I understand you're at the Avalon Estate Apartments. As you come out your gate, turn right, my restaurant is about a half-mile down on your right, 1341

Central Ave. I assume you don't drive yet, so it will be about a half-hour walk for you."

"I'll be there, sir, what time would you like me to arrive?"

"Well, the first thing every morning, I meet with my staff, making sure everybody's there and everything is under control. Things settle down for me around 10 o'clock, how's that sound to you?"

"Ten o'clock is perfect sir, I'll be there."

"Oh, one other thing, everybody calls me Chip. I'll see you tomorrow."

When the call ended, he was still holding the phone in his hand, unable to believe what just happened. "Kevin," he said smiling, "you're not going to believe this. I think I have a job beginning tomorrow!"

"I know, I heard, congratulations. The first chapter of your new life has begun. Let's have dinner, then watch a little TV, how's that sound?" Opening the freezer, he took a visual inventory. "Tonight, I'm going to suggest what I call the bachelor special," he said withdrawing two Swanson TV dinners. "One chicken, one meatloaf, which would you prefer?"

"It makes no difference to me, I like everything," Jimmy said, while leaning on the countertop, studying Kevin's every move.

He removed two placemats from a drawer, placing them on the table along with napkins, forks and two glasses of ice water.

Kevin cut off a piece of meatloaf and was halfway to his mouth when he noticed Jimmy, again saying a silent prayer.

After finishing their meal, Kevin rinsed the glasses and silverware in the sink while he discarded the aluminum trays in the trash.

"I wish I had some dessert to offer you but I ate the last of my ice cream yesterday. So, what you say, we watch a little television before turning in?"

"That's a good idea, I'm too excited to sleep anyway. I can't wait till tomorrow."

As was his habit, Kevin turned on channel 5, the six o'clock news. Jimmy had no idea what the news man was talking about, neither the people, nor the location of which the news reporter spoke meant anything to him, as he was totally unfamiliar with the area.

"One of the first things I need to do," Jimmy said, "is explore the surrounding neighborhood and beyond."

"I totally understand," said Kevin, "it would be like me watching the news in Czechoslovakia.

Slowly but surely watching TV will help you to catch up."

After the news, Kevin switched over to a show called *All in The Family*. Kevin noticed that almost everything this guy named Archie said brought laughter from the audience.

Jimmy listened intently, but could not see the humor. He noticed Kevin laughed hysterically throughout the program.

"Archie is some character isn't he, Jimmy?" Kevin asked, still chuckling.

"I must say, I find some things funny, but being isolated for so long, I find this humor difficult to understand."

"Like I said before, everything will eventually fall into place. Don't rush it, just let it happen."

When the show ended, Kevin stood, stretched and yawned, "I think I'm going to hit the rack. I'll close my door so the sound won't bother me, just turn the TV off when you're finished."

"Ahh, before you go, could you show me how to work that thing you're holding?"

"Oh, I'm sorry, this is a remote." Standing beside Jimmy, holding the remote in his left hand and pointing with his right, he said, "Look, this is the on-off switch, this is the volume and arrows up and down to select your channel."

"Sounds simple enough, thanks for your help and patience."

When Kevin left, Jimmy turned the volume completely off and practiced what he just learned. Realizing that he should get a good night's rest before his interview tomorrow, he decided to call it a night.

When he entered his room, he still couldn't help but marvel at the fact that his door locked from the inside, under his control, instead of the other way around. He took another moment, with his hands on his hips, slowly turned 360° saying a short prayer, thanking God for all his blessings.

Climbing into bed, he felt the cool comfort of the sheets and pillowcases. So much different than the rough texture of what he had been accustomed. In spite of his most pleasant surroundings, he couldn't relax. Sleep was intermittent and restless. Several times he awakened, looked at the clock, only to realize scarcely an hour had passed.

At 7:15 he heard movement coming from the other room. The shower was so invigorating, it was all he could do to turn it off and exit. On the countertop he saw where Kevin had placed various items, shaving cream, deodorant, toothbrush, toothpaste, and a razor along with a bottle of old spice aftershave lotion. This was the first time in his life that he was permitted to shave alone and keep the razor in his possession.

He stepped out of his room to see Kevin banging away on a typewriter at his desk just off the kitchen.

"Good morning, I heard you moving around, so I left milk and cereal on the counter. Bowls are in the cabinet above you and silverware in the drawer to the left. As time goes by, you'll learn the art of preparing bacon, eggs, pancakes or anything else."

Jimmy took a bowl from the cupboard, filling it with something called Frosted Flakes. He returned the milk to the refrigerator, stood there gathering his thoughts before carrying his breakfast to the table.

" I want to thank you, Kevin, for the stuff you left in the bathroom. I want you to know I'm keeping track of everything so I can pay you back. I'm looking forward to my job interview this morning. I'm anxious to begin paying my own way. Based on my phone conversation with Mr. Francis last night, things are looking pretty good."

Kevin stopped typing, and in a friendly but authoritative voice said, "I've told you before, don't worry about that, besides, a certain family member of yours in Colorado sent me an advance toward your expenses. When we get back this evening from visiting your mother, we'll stop at the mall and pick up a few extra things to get you through until you get your first paycheck."

"My first paycheck, that has a nice ring to it. Since I don't have to be at the restaurant for another three hours, I'd like to go out and walk the neighborhood, is that okay with you?"

"I think that would be a good idea, but you don't need my permission. I know it's going to take you a while, and if it's okay, I'll continue to remind you. Enjoy your walk. Remember our address is Central Avenue. If you get turned around, look for the large water tower directly across the street from the complex."

"Oh, and one more thing, wait here. I have something for you," he said, opening the middle drawer of his desk. He handed Jimmy a small black box. It's an inexpensive Timex watch, but you're going to need it. Remember, we have a hospital visit this evening. We'll have to leave here by five."

"Thanks, I never thought of that. Where I came from, time meant nothing."

CHAPTER FIFTEEN

Jimmy stepped out the door, into the bright sunlight, where he stopped, stretched, slowly looking around. He felt like he had to pinch himself to make sure he wasn't dreaming. While walking down Central Avenue, he was overwhelmed by what seemed to be a hundred different sounds, each one vying for his attention. Car horns, buses, a dog barking in the distance, and a very loud motorcycle, all blending with the chatter of people talking. For a while, it was very uncomfortable, but soon settled into his subconscious. He found himself reading all the signs along the way, Top 40 Records, Carlson's Appliances, New-2-U Thrift Store. He was again overcome by a euphoric feeling, wanting to take everything in simultaneously. Up ahead a sign read, Britannica Gardens, next right. He soon found himself in a beautiful park next to a small pond surrounded by a multitude of flowers. He watched a teenager throwing a tennis ball to his dog, a young mother pushing a little boy on a swing. Up ahead, an elderly man sat on a bench, reading a newspaper. Jimmy's mind traveled back to the article about the prisoner of war who fantasized about talking to people in the park. But this is real. He felt compelled to say good morning.

The old man seemed surprised that a youngster would take time to speak to him. Laying his paper aside, he looked up, smiling. "Well, good morning yourself young man, it's a perfect day for walk in the park isn't it?"

"Yes, it is. I've never been here before. What a beautiful view."

"I come here every day, nothing else to do since I retired. I feel like my only purpose is to consume oxygen since my wife passed away two years ago."

A feeling of sympathy, or perhaps empathy, came over Jimmy at that moment. "Do you mind if I sit for a while? I have a little time to kill."

"Please do, I don't often get company. Besides, there's no good news in this paper anyway. If it weren't for the crossword puzzle, I wouldn't waste my money on it."

The more they spoke, the more candid they became with each other. The old man talked about everything from the Great Depression to his job as a brakeman on the B&O Railroad. How he lost his son in the Vietnam War, what a wonderful wife he had. Jimmy felt very much at ease sharing his past with this stranger.

Looking at his watch, he said, "Oh my gosh, I've gotta go, my appointment is in thirty minutes. I'll stop by and see you again; I've enjoyed our conversation."

"I would like that. I'm here every day about this time. My name is Howard, what's your name?"

"It's Jimmy, Jimmy Simmons," he said looking at his watch, shaking the old man's hand, before breaking into a jog back toward Central Avenue.

Walking down the street, he began to rehearse what he might say during the interview. Never applying for a job before, he was at a total loss. He did however, remember what Chaplain Mike used to say. When at a loss for words, listen. Looking up to his right, a neon sign glowed, Garden of Eaten. As he entered the front door, a smiling young lady approached him.

"Would you like a table or booth she asked?"

Feeling somewhat intimidated, he replied, "Um, I have an appointment with Mr. Frances at 10 o'clock. My name is Jimmy Simmons."

"Have a seat, I'll let him know you're here."

A few moments later Jimmy watched a man appearing to be in his early sixties come through the swinging doors from the kitchen. He was tall, slim, approximately 6'3" tall, with a full head of snow-white hair. He moved with the energy of an eighteen-year-old as he approached him.

"You're early, I like that, punctuality is important in this business," he said, extending his hand.

His firm handshake and genuine smile immediately put him at ease.

"Let's go to my office and discuss the position," he said, leading the way back through the double doors. "Would you like a cup of coffee, Coke, anything?" he asked, motioning him to have a seat.

"No sir, I'm fine," he said, taking his seat.

"Okay, but remember, my name is Chip. There were too many Mikes in my family growing up. People often said I was a *chip off the old block*. My dad was a great man so being compared to him was an incredible compliment. Thus, Chip became the name I answer to. Now, with that out of the way, let me explain how things work around here. All new hires begin at the bottom, moving up as they progress in the job. The pay is minimum wage, with an evaluation after thirty days. We believe in teamwork, so all gratuities are divided equally among the waitstaff as well as their backup, dishwashers and busboys. In most cases, the gratuities equal the minimum wage. You will shadow Billy Weber, who is being promoted to the waitstaff, for the first few days. Everybody works five days, rotating each week to ensure everybody gets their share of weekends. Do you have any questions?"

"No sir. . . er, I mean Chip, I'm just happy to have a job so I can carry my own weight."

"Excellent attitude, Jimmy, let's take a walk. I'll introduce you to our people." It impressed Jimmy that he called all the help by their first name, while offering an occasional complement.

"Jimmy," he said, "this is our executive chef, Matteo Romano. Matteo is not only the best chef in the city, if not the state, he is also the author of a best-selling cookbook called Matteo's Kitchen.

They made their way through the restaurant as he introduced Jimmy to Karen, boasting that she was one of the most popular servers they had. She was constantly being requested by their most demanding customers. He introduced Jimmy to every person in the building, who, without exception, showed a genuine fondness for their boss.

While walking him to the door, Chip said, "Billy is anxious to begin his new position as a waiter, so can you possibly start tomorrow?"

"Yes, I would love to start tomorrow. What time? How should I dress?"

"There's no dress code, you look good the way you are. You'll be wearing a green Garden of Eaten apron. Be sure to wear comfortable shoes as you'll be doing a lot of walking and standing."

Jimmy walked back to the apartment. His mind was racing, going over every detail of his meeting with Chip and getting the job. Before he knew it, he was home. Entering the apartment, he saw a note Kevin left him saying there was a fruit salad in the refrigerator. But he was far too excited to eat. Not only was he elated about his first job, but also excited for the first ever visit to his mother that evening with Kevin. So, he walked into his room, and lay on the bed, opening his Bible.

* * *

While turning into the main gate at Pittsfield Psychiatric Hospital, Kevin saw Jimmy had his eyes closed, rubbing his hands on his thighs, obviously very nervous.

"You okay?" he asked him while reaching over and gently patting his shoulder.

Jimmy opened his eyes, hesitating for a second, and replied, "Do you realize this may be the most memorable day of my life? I get a job and meet my mother, both for the first time ever."

Looking at the building entrance, he continued, "This place used to be my home. Today is the first time I've seen it from the outside. It's been quite a day of firsts."

While checking in at the front desk, the young attendant could not take her eyes off Jimmy. She had heard the name and seen the face, but couldn't make the connection.

"Good afternoon, Mr. Lankford, you know where the room is so there's no need for an escort. Please don't forget to sign out before you leave."

Kevin walked into Rachel's room before realizing that Jimmy was no longer with him. He walked back into the hallway, finding him leaning with his back against the wall, his eyes closed and arms crossed at his chest.

"Hey, what's wrong?" he said, gripping his shoulders while holding him at arm's length.

"I don't know. I'm so nervous I can't think straight. I don't even know what to call her."

"You can call her Mom, she's your mother, but don't worry about that right now, just follow my lead, everything will be okay. Come on, it will get easier with time."

She had her back to the door, staring out the window, as usual. Kevin gently turned her chair around, hoping that by removing any distractions, they might possibly get some kind of reaction from her. He pulled up the chair that was next to her bed and told Jimmy to have a seat. He then opened the small closet and retrieved the folding chair for himself.

He gently lifted her right hand in his, saying, "This is Jimmy, your son."

At that moment, he was elated to see her eyes slowly turn and look straight at him, as if she knew who he was. Jimmy looked at Kevin, his lost expression indicating what should I do now?

Kevin motioned for him to hold her other hand, which he did. Looking directly into her eyes and smiling, he said, "Hi Mom, I'm your son. I'm so happy to see you."

It was somewhat awkward as both men attempted to make conversation. Kevin did notice her eyes moved back and forth to each of them as they spoke.

Looking at his watch, Kevin announced, "We've got to go now, but we'll be back to see you as often as we can."

As they stood to leave, they got the most unexpected reaction from Rachel. She squeezed both of their hands, pulling them toward her as if to say don't leave.

Jimmy sat back down. Breaking the silence while patting her hand he said, "We have to go now, but we will be back."

She loosened her grip on their hands as if she understood.

Kevin turned her chair back toward the window, giving her a smile and a wave of his hand.

Jimmy patted her right shoulder and said, "Bye Mom, I'll be back soon."

Kevin noticed that he was having as much difficulty leaving the room, as he did when he entered.

On the drive home Kevin spoke nonstop, rambling on about Rachel showing emotion. "I'm telling you, there's hope for her. She is in there. I believe one day she'll come out. The way she looked at you, her eyes following you, the way she hung onto your hand when we were ready to leave."

"But," Jimmy countered, "her eyes followed you as well, and she clung to your hand just like mine, how do you explain that?"

"I can't explain it, but I'm telling you, I'm not imagining this, there's definitely something going on. I've heard stories about maternal instincts women have regarding their children. I'm no expert in the field, but I know one. I have a good friend in Colorado who teaches psychiatry at the university. He's written books on the subject of human instincts. I'm going to call him tomorrow. I don't trust these quacks in the state mental hospitals, but I do trust Dr. Evans. I've seen improvements, nothing major like today when she wouldn't let go of our hands, that was absolutely unbelievable. The funny thing is, I've been somewhat of a skeptic my whole life, but this is different. Call it a gut feeling or overly optimistic, something deep inside of me says I'm right."

Walking into their apartment, Kevin said, "I'm in no mood to cook tonight, not even a Swanson TV dinner. So, let's have a pizza delivered, what would you like on it?"

Shrugging his shoulders, he answered, "I don't know, I've never eaten pizza."

"Well, you're in for treat, I'll order a super deluxe, pepperoni, sausage, peppers, onions and mushrooms, everything but the kitchen sink. You're gonna love it, you're also going to need some Tums if you plan on sleeping tonight," he said, chuckling.

"I do need a good night's sleep. Remember, tomorrow is my first day on the job, so, whatever Tums are, I hope you have some."

Finishing the last piece of pizza, Jimmy said, "That was absolutely delicious. I've never tasted anything like it."

"How about we watch the news to see what's going on in the world around us?"

"Thanks, but I have some reading to do, so I think I'll just take a shower and go to bed."

"Hold on a second, I'll be right back," Kevin said, going into his room. A few seconds later he returned with a bottle of Tums. He handed them to Jimmy, but not before pouring a few in his own hand. "If you wake up with indigestion, chew a few of these and you'll be good to go. "Oh, one thing" he said, removing his wallet from his back pocket. He handed him a twenty-dollar bill. "Always keep a little cash in your pocket, you never know when you might need it."

Jimmy held up both hands, leaning back in a defensive position. "No, you've done enough. It's an easy walk to work and my meals are supplied by the restaurant."

"Look, you could get caught in a torrential downpour on the way to work, and need to take a bus. Besides, you can pay me back after a couple paychecks, so take this," he said, stuffing it into Jimmy's shirt pocket.

"Thanks, but remember, I'm keeping track of all this. I will pay you back every penny as soon as possible."

"Fine, I know you will. Good luck on the job, I'm anxious to hear about it tomorrow evening."

Jimmy read from the book of Acts in his Bible and was touched by how Paul and Silas sang hymns while in prison, and how a great earth-quake caused the prison doors to open. Remembering what Kevin said about the pizza causing indigestion, he chewed up four Tums before turning off the light, hoping to get a decent night's sleep. He slept fitfully, most likely due to the visit with his mother along with his apprehension about starting a new job in the morning.

* * *

He arrived at the restaurant a half-hour early and entered through the back door as instructed. He was greeted by a young man approximately his age.

"You must be Jimmy," the young man said, while shaking his hand and handing him a green apron. "I'm Billy Weber. It looks like we will be working together for the next two days. I think you're gonna like it here. Everybody is easy to get along with, as long as you do your job, and remember, we're a team. I've enjoyed doing what I do, but the promotion to waiter means more money in the paycheck. You do a good job and you'll be promoted as well. Chip is a great guy to work for, always fair, considerate of his employees, always promoting from within."

"Yes, I know," Jimmy replied. "During my interview he made me feel like a member of the team. I'm ready to go when you are, so what's next?"

"First thing, put your apron on and follow me. Our two main responsibilities are to clear and clean the tables immediately because the customer turnover is nonstop. Second, and most important, always be polite. Sometimes the customers are not so polite, but we must always smile and show respect. When the tables are wiped down and reset, we wash, sanitize and place all the plates, cups, and silverware within reach of the cooks. Things are beginning to pick up out there, so let's get started."

He played follow the leader for the first few hours. When things slowed down after lunch, Billy said, "Now, we switch roles. You lead and I'll follow."

Jimmy picked it up quickly, doing everything Billy did, though with less speed and confidence. When the shift was over, Billy complimented him on how well he did. "Maybe one or two more days, you'll be ready. But remember, if you have any questions, I am here to help in any way I can."

Just as he predicted, Jimmy became very

proficient at his job. In just a few days Chip received many very complimentary remarks about the new kid. He soon gained confidence, looking forward to going to work every day.

On his two days off, he continued to meet his new friend Howard at the park bench with coffee and donuts. Howard seemed to live for those two days each week. Jimmy on the other hand felt personal fulfillment, doing what he felt was his purpose. Often times, he hardly spoke at all. He sat looking straight ahead, tossing bits of his donut to a family of squirrels, while listening to Howard reminisce about his job on the railroad, losing his wife to cancer and his son in Vietnam. Jimmy heard the stories so many times, he could repeat them verbatim, but that was okay. Harold needed to talk, and it was his job to listen.

In the evenings, he and Kevin visited his mom at the hospital. With every visit there was another victory. One day as they walked into her room, she greeted them with a beautiful, genuine smile. Another time, as they were about to leave, they observed her eyes welled up with tears. Kevin received some encouraging advice from his professor friend in Colorado. This advice proved valuable. Their interactions with

Rachel were beginning to show encouraging results.

One evening while returning from work, Jimmy found Kevin feverishly pounding on his typewriter. "Are we going to visit my mom this evening? "Jimmy asked, while pouring himself a glass of milk and sitting at the table across from Kevin.

"Can't make it today, Jimmy, the magazine is on my case, the deadline for this story is in two weeks and I have to wrap this thing up. My dream as a writer is to one day produce a best-selling novel, then I can set my own deadlines. You know your way around by now, the bus stop is one block north, get off at 32nd, turn right at the bank, the hospital is about two hundred yards ahead. I wish I could join you tonight, but I've got to get this done."

"No problem Kevin, I need to find my way around this town. Every day is a new experience. I'll see you in a few hours," he said as he walked out the door.

A half-hour later, he was walking down the hall toward his mother's room, feeling confident, somewhat proud of himself. He was beginning to feel like a regular ordinary citizen, rather than a ward of the state of Ohio.

As he walked into her room, she was sitting facing the door, giving him a beautiful smile as he arrived, but not seeing Kevin her expression turned to confusion as she held up two fingers, as if to say, there should be two of you.

"Kevin couldn't be here today Mom, but he will see you next time." He noticed her expression change from confusion to acceptance. He walked over to retrieve a chair near her bed. As he turned back toward her, he was immediately alarmed at her change of expression again, to a look of sheer terror. He pivoted and hurried into the hall to see who had walked past her open door. He caught a glimpse of a tall man in a business suit closing the door behind him. He didn't see his face, but knew it couldn't be a nurse or attendant since they all wore white. This person definitely had the authority to open locked doors. Whoever it was had put the fear of God into his mother. One way or another, he was determined to discover the man's identity.

Re-entering the room, he could see his mother was still visibly shaken. She reached out both hands to him as if looking for comfort. He sat down in front of her, took both her hands in his, softly saying, "It's all right mom, I'm here now, you are safe, everything is going to be all right."

Jimmy was quiet for a moment gathering his thoughts, remembering that Kevin's professor friend had suggested they discuss events that occurred during the years which she would be most familiar prior to her head injury. He spent the next hour talking about some of the events that could have taken place in her teenage years, including singing some of the popular songs and movies of that time.   Jimmy was quiet for a moment gathering his thoughts, remembering that Kevin's professor friend had suggested they discuss events that occurred during the years which she would be most familiar prior to her head injury. He spent the next hour talking about some of the events that could have taken place in her teenage years, including singing some of the popular songs and movies of that time. By the time he was ready to leave, Rachel seemed to have recovered from whatever, or whoever, had caused such panic. Jimmy turned her chair back toward the window, kissed her on top of the head saying, "I love you Mom, I'll see you Thursday evening."

While approaching the exit, he was pleasantly surprised to see Anna Frances leaving the building. "Anna," he shouted, "what are you doing here so late?" Before she could answer, he added, "I can't tell you how much I appreciate your helping me get that job; what a nice boss Chip is."

"Jimmy," she exclaimed," it's so good to see you." Giving him a warm hug, then holding him at arm's length, she said, "You are the success story of the century. I'm so proud to be a part of it, as I'm sure Dale, Kevin and many others.

"You asked, why am I here? Well, the Emperor decided to hold what he considered a very important meeting, with me and creepy..., I mean Kyle, from Bainbridge. I know it isn't very professional of me to disparage my superiors. But, you more than anyone else know what I'm talking about. The two of us, Kyle and me, like good little students, sat in front of his monstrous desk, listening to a lecture we've heard many times before. He sat there holding one of his famous Meerschaum pipes, while going through his usual hand motions making his point. I still don't know why we were there. He reviewed things we learned years ago in orientation. But, as my dad used to say, the boss isn't always right, but he's always the boss."

Jimmy laughed. "Better you than me. Sounds like you had a stressful day. I don't know how you deal with it all. Well, I'd better get going, I spent longer visiting with my mom than I had planned and I have work tomorrow, thanks to you."

It occurred to Anna that Jimmy was alone. Looking around she said, "By the way, where's Kevin?"

"He's busy working on his article. Sometimes I feel guilty, that he spends so much time worrying about me, he gets behind in his own work. I took a bus here today."

"A bus? I go right past your apartment on my way home. Let's go, I'll drop you off."

Jimmy thanked Anna for the ride and hurried inside, anxious to share the events of the evening with Kevin. Upon hearing the account of Rachel's panic episode along with creepy Kyle being in town, Kevin decided that it may be time to re-open a twenty-four-year-old criminal case. Tomorrow he planned to make a personal visit to the County Sheriff's Department.

* * *

The lobby of the Sheriff's Department was virtually empty when Kevin walked in, with the exception of the lady behind the reception desk. She was so focused on what she was reading, she didn't appear to notice Kevin's presence. When he intentionally coughed, she looked up, startled.

"Oh my, you caught me by surprise," she said. "How can I help you?"

"I'd like to know who in the department I might speak with regarding a crime that was committed over twenty-five years ago."

Squinting at the screen of her desktop computer, she entered the words cold cases. "Let's see," she said, running her finger down the screen, "that would be Lieut. Ryan Murphy. Lieut. Murphy is conducting read off and should be finished within the next thirty minutes. Please have a seat. I'll let him know you're here."

Kevin sat down in a chair next to an end table which contained the monthly Sheriff Department magazine called *The Guardian.* The magazine contained pictures of recent retirees, important cases that had not been solved, along with mugshots of wanted fugitives. While reading an article on the Deputy- of-the-Month, Kevin heard footsteps. Looking up, he saw a man in uniform approaching. He looked to be in his middle 50s, about 5'10" tall with reddish-brown hair and a ruddy complexion. Assuming that he must be Lieut. Murphy, Kevin stood up, meeting him halfway across the lobby.

"Good morning," Murphy said, extending his hand. "Marianne said that you're looking for the cold case guy. That would be me. how can I help you?"

Kevin was impressed with his firm handshake and direct eye contact. Instinctively, he felt, this is the kind of guy I can feel comfortable around. "Well sir," Kevin began, "I'd like to discuss a rape that took place over twenty-five years ago at Pittsfield Psychiatric Hospital."

At the mention of rape and Pittsfield, Lieut. Murphy's expression indicated that a nerve had been touched. "Let's go into my office so we can talk in private. Please follow me."

His office was sparsely decorated. On his credenza was a photograph Kevin presumed to be of his family, along with a plaque reading Deputy-of-the- Month and a bowling trophy. On a corner table was a Mr. Coffee with some Styrofoam cups. "I drink mine black," he said. "If you want cream and sugar, I suppose I could round up some."

"Thank you, Lieutenant, I like my coffee black also."

"Standby for a minute, I'll be right back."

The lieutenant returned shortly carrying a box labeled cold cases. Placing it on his desk, he thumbed through several files before pulling one out that read, *Simmons*. Looking up at Kevin he said, "This case has been haunting me for years. I thought it would remain in the dead files forever."

"So, you're familiar with the case. Are you at liberty to tell me about it?"

The lieutenant removed his glasses, began cleaning them slowly, appearing to be formulating his remarks. "I was a young buck then, with less than a year on the job, when this whole thing took place. The sheriff at that time was Jack Pierce. I always thought he was more of a politician than a law enforcement officer, but as a rookie, there was nothing I could do."

"What did he do, if I may ask?"

"He did next to nothing, that's what I had a problem with. He listened to the hospital administrator, who assured him that their internal investigation turned up nothing. In those days forensic science was limited to fingerprints, autopsies, blood types and ballistics. Today we have a lot more tools to work with. The best thing that ever came along in law enforcement is DNA. A drop of sweat, a single hair, or a microscopic fiber from a victim's clothing can put a person in prison for life. Oh, don't get me wrong, the department sent detectives over there, who interviewed a few people and went through the motions, which in my opinion were halfhearted."

Opening the file, he withdrew three sheets of paper. "Look at this, three lousy sheets of paper do not make a thorough investigation. I always believed in my heart that justice was not done for that poor, young girl. I'm not saying the Sheriff did anything wrong. What I am saying is this case deserved more attention than it got."

"Is there any possibility that the case can be reopened?" Kevin asked.

"I'm currently in charge of cold cases. I can reopen any case if I have probable cause. I'm sure you didn't show up here today without specific reason in mind. So, what do you know that might be helpful?"

"I'm close friends with the man who was born to Rachel following the rape. As you know, she had twins. Her other son lives in Colorado Springs and is a personal friend of mine. His family is well connected politically and they're determined to find out who raped Rachel Sim-

mons. For many years she has been in a co-
matose state. Over the last several months, her
son Jimmy has been visiting her. I can't explain
it, call it maternal instincts, or whatever you
want, but Rachel is showing improvement since
Jimmy began visiting her. She is beginning to
show emotion, eye movements, smiles and even
tears. The other day somebody walked past her
open door and Jimmy saw terror in her eyes, total panic. He ran into the hall only to see a man
dressed in a business suit exit the pod. She
had never shown the slightest fear of anybody
prior to this time. I've had my suspicions about
a certain individual who heads up another facility. That individual was at Pittsfield on that
day, and possessed a master key to open any
door in the building.

"Who is that person?" Lieut. Murphy asked,
leaning forward. "What's his name?"

"His name is Kyle Phillips, administrator at
Bainbridge Psychiatric Hospital for the criminally insane."

"That's something. Not a lot, but enough to
possibly reopen the case. I'm going to need a
few days to plan strategy and make sure I have
my ducks in a row before visiting Mr. Phillips. I
imagine I should have something by next Tues-

day. I'll keep you informed. If you think of anything else, you can call me here anytime."

"Kevin stood, handing him a business card. This number is my answering service. I call in several times a day. If there's anything else you need, please don't hesitate to call that number."

Kevin left the building believing that Lieut. Murphy just might be the person to finally uncover the truth after all these years.

* * *

The sun shining through his bedroom window brought Jimmy from a dreamless sleep. Today was one of the few Saturdays off from work. He quietly walked out of his room, careful not to disturb Kevin, who was either sleeping or working on his article. Pouring himself a cup of coffee, he picked up a newspaper and sat down in the La-Z-Boy recliner in the corner of the living room.

Taking a sip, he was reminded of that day just three months ago when he tasted coffee for the first time ever. Mental hospitals had a policy not to serve coffee, which is a stimulant, the last thing they needed in their sometimes-chaotic environment. After the first taste, he wondered how in the world people got hooked on the stuff. However, he decided, if I'm going to live in the real world, I should probably get used to it.

Before long, it became a regular morning routine. Glancing at the sports page, the headline read, *Tribe Wins in Extra Innings.* He didn't know much about baseball, but his friend Howard loved the Cleveland Indians. He decided to spend some extra time with Howard today. His eyes drifted to the date on the newspaper. It was June 3rd. Something about that date caught his attention. Holy smokes, he said to himself, today is my birthday. Birthdays were rarely, if ever, celebrated in psychiatric institutions. His first instinct was to tell Kevin, but he decided to wait until Kevin returned.

Stepping out of the apartment, the warm balmy day lifted his spirits further. On the way to the park, he remembered Howard's habit of working the crossword puzzle in the newspaper. On impulse, he walked into a Walgreens drugstore and purchased a book of 100 crossword puzzles. He smiled with anticipation of giving Howard a gift. The joy on Howard's face at receiving that little book reminded Jimmy of a Bible verse he read just the night before, it is more blessed to give than to receive.

"That's so thoughtful of you," Howard said, lightly rubbing his fingers over the book cover, then turning it over and reading the back page. "This should keep me busy for a while," he said, smiling, "but what's the occasion?"

"It's a birthday present, Howard," Jimmy replied.

"But it's not my birthday, I was born in December."

"I know, today is my birthday and I felt like buying somebody a birthday present."

"Well, happy birthday young man, and thank you so much for the book. Since it's your birthday," he said opening the book, "you can help me with the first puzzle."

After completing three puzzles, Jimmy looked at his watch saying, "It's been fun, Howard. I'd like to sit here longer, but I have a very important date this evening with a very lovely lady."

Howard looked at him with a sly grin, "And who would that lucky lady be?"

"That lucky lady is my mother, the person who gave birth to me, twenty-five years ago today. Save some of those puzzles for our next visit," Jimmy said, standing, "I had a great time, I'll see you soon."

* * *

As the two men entered the hospital lobby, Kevin saw a stack of monthly magazines called the *Buckeye State News*, which he picked up out of curiosity.

Rachel smiled as the two men walked into her room. Then, she did something that totally shocked them. Looking up at them, she crossed her hands over her heart, then, pointing an index finger at each of them, silently mouthed the words, "I love you."

Both men approached her. Kneeling down at eye level, each held one of her hands, repeating in unison, "We love you too." Kevin and Jimmy looked at each other speechless.

Kevin whispered, "It's working, Jimmy. I knew it. Dr. Evans was right, our visits and personal interactions are making a difference. We need to visit with her as much as possible. There's no telling what could happen next."

What happened next was startling! Kevin decided to share with her some pictures in the magazine he'd picked up in the lobby. The front page had a picture of several brand-new Highway Patrol vehicles, accompanied by a short article. Kevin turned the page to find a group picture of several men in business suits. Before he could read the headlines, Rachel pulled the magazine from his hand, throwing it on the floor.

"It's that same look, Kevin," Jimmy blurted. "See the fear in her eyes, just like that time the stranger walked past her door. What was it that she saw in the magazine?"

Kevin picked the magazine off the floor, opening it to page two. The headline read, *State Mental Health Executives*. It was a picture of about twenty hospital administrators from around the state. In the back row, center, was the familiar face of Kyle Phillips.

"It's okay, don't worry, it's only a picture, we're here with you, Mom," Jimmy said. Holding her face in his hands, he repeated, "I love you, Mom. We won't let anything happen to you. I promise."

It took Rachel a while to settle down. Soon, her smile was back. They both gave her a gentle hug, smiled, and waved goodbye, promising to be back real soon.

On the ride back home, Kevin waved the magazine, saying, "I need to take this to Lieutenant Murphy on Monday. What happened back there, tells me my suspicions about that creep just might be valid."

They rode along in silence for a while until Jimmy said, "Kevin, I need to ask you a question. It's something that has been bothering me."

"Sure, what is it," he replied.

"I hope you don't take this wrong, but I can't help thinking there is something you haven't told me."

"Like what?" Kevin asked.

"You know my twin brother and claim to be close friends with him," he said, pausing to collect his thoughts and form his next question. "Why is it that I have not been able to speak to him on the phone, or get a letter from him, or even see a photograph? That's really been bothering me."

"Jimmy, there's a reason, and you'll have the answer very soon. As a matter of fact, you will see him in person, shortly."

In an emotional voice, he pressed, "When am I going to see him, next week, next month?"

Kevin reached over, patted his shoulder saying, "Soon, very soon.," He smiled. Jimmy's expression showed he wasn't exactly satisfied with the answer, but decided to let it go for now.

Kevin unlocked the door, motioning Jimmy to go in ahead of him.

Jimmy froze in the doorway as a chorus of people greeted him with shouts of happy birthday, then broke into the happy birthday song, a song nobody had ever sung to him. While in near total shock, he looked around the room. The first person he saw was Dale Karsten with a lady by his side, obviously his wife. Then Pete Fetzer, Anna Frances, his boss, Chip, stood next to Dale. Somebody had even gone to the park and brought his friend Howard to the party. Looking around he saw a beautifully decorated cake with twenty-five candles and the words *happy birthday, Jimmy and Gerry*. With tears of joy running down his cheeks, all he could say was, "Thank you, thank you, I don't know what to say. This is one of the best days of my life."

Looking down at the birthday cake on the table, he read out loud, "Happy Birthday Jimmy and Gerry. Turning to Kevin he said, "The only thing in the world that could make this day perfect, is if Gerry were here with us."

Kevin spoke up saying, "Gerry is here with us."

"Are you kidding me? Gerry's here! Where is he?" He made a 360° turn, looking again at every face in the room. Where is he?"

"I think you better sit down for this Jimmy."

Kevin, looking around the room said, "Let's all take a seat, I have a story to tell."

The entire room went silent with anticipation.

Kevin again motioned with both palms down, repeated, "Everyone please take a seat.

"Friends," he began, "as you know, I'm a writer for the national magazine called *The World Today*. I'm currently working on an article entitled twins separated at birth. What you don't know is that I personally am a twin who was separated at birth."

This brought a wave of murmurs and whispers from those in the room. Waiting until the room was quiet, he continued. "You all know me as Kevin Langford, but again, what you don't know is, my legal name is Gerald Rawlins. However, the name on my birth certificate is. . ." he paused for a second, "Gerald Simmons. I am Jimmy's biological twin brother."

Gasps erupted throughout the room, while Jimmy, leaning forward with his hands clasped behind his head, sobbed uncontrollably.

Kevin clutched his shoulders, pulled him out of his chair and looked him in the eyes. "I told you this afternoon while returning from visiting our mother, that you would see your twin brother soon. I hope I'm not a disappointment to you. So many times, I wanted to tell you everything."

"Why, why didn't you tell me?"

"If people knew my real identity, they would get emotionally involved. As Kevin Langford, everybody saw me as a neutral reporter and were completely candid."

Jimmy, wiping his tears on his shirt sleeves while struggling to gain his composure said, "You have been so kind to me. I prayed every night that when I finally met my brother, he would be somebody just like you. My prayers have been answered. You are my brother. I believe, that our mother sensed this all along."

As the reunited twins embraced, the room broke into thunderous applause. There was no shortage of tears from the guests.

Dale took it upon himself to light the twenty-five candles and lead one more course of happy birthday. Together, Gerald and Jimmy Simmons, blew them out while everybody cheered.

Kevin tapped a wineglass with his fork to get everyone's attention.

"On behalf of Jimmy and me, I want to thank all of you for coming and making our birthday so special. We'll never forget you. I also want you to know the story isn't over, not by a long-shot. My brother and I have a big job ahead of us. First and foremost is to get our mother out of Pittsfield and into a suitable facility. I know I'm speaking for Jimmy as well as myself. We will not rest until her attacker is brought to justice."

When all the guests had gone, the two brothers sat at the table facing each other. Neither could stop smiling.

"What a day," Kevin said, holding his coffee cup as if making a toast. His brother repeated the gesture saying, "I'm at a loss for words. I always knew, if I kept a positive attitude and had faith in God, things would work out. But I never, in my wildest dreams, imagined it would be this good."

"There's one other thing I'd like you to think about, Jimmy," Kevin said, pausing for a few seconds before continuing. Would you consider relocating to Colorado? When we get mom out of Pittsfield, and we will get her out, I'm sure the three of us would want to remain geographically close. I grew up in Colorado Springs, which is the only home I've ever known."

Without a second's hesitation, Jimmy replied., "I would absolutely love it. With the exception of a few foster families, the only home I knew was the inside of some state-run institution. It's a big world. I'm anxious to see as much of it as possible. Like you, I want us to stay close. Besides, Colorado Springs sounds like a wonderful place."

"I had a feeling you would agree, but I wanted it to be your decision. Speaking of decisions, now that your nightmare is behind you, what are your plans going forward?"

Jimmy remained silent momentarily, attempting to prioritize his goals.

"I've been thinking about that a lot lately. First, it's very important that I get a driver's license. I love my job, but don't intend to be a dishwasher the rest of my life, and I can't continue to depend on others for transportation. I realize money isn't everything, but if I'm going to move up the economic ladder, I'll need further education. I did some research and found a night class being offered at the library not far from here. I've decided to sign up for GED classes, then, Lord willing, I'll look into some college courses. I'm not exactly sure of what career to pursue, but I do know I want to make a difference in the lives of hurting and hopeless people."

Kevin's face showed an expression of admiration as he nodded in agreement. "My dad used to say, when you find the job you love, you'll never work a day in your life. Considering what you've been through, I have no doubt that you will touch and change the lives of many people in the future. I truly believe that is your purpose. There is one thing I'd like you to do."

"Of course, What is that?"

"I know it may take a little while and some practice, but please, from now on, I'd like you to call me Jerry, my birth name, my real name. That will make our reunion official."

"I will," he said, smiling. "From this day on, you are now my older brother Jerry."

"Ah ha, I never thought of that," he replied in an authoritative voice. "Don't forget, I'm the patriarch of this family. So, as leader, I suggest we hit the rack. My article is finished and delivered. Tomorrow is Sunday, so there's very little we can do except plan our strategy for the future. With that he stood up, walked to the sink and rinsed his cup before saying, "Good night, good night brother."

"Good night Kevin, . . . I mean Jerry, I'll see you in the morning."

He walked into his room, pivoted and walked

back out. "Jerry, I've been wanting to go to that little church by the park, would you like to go with me?"

Jerry wasn't sure how he felt about that and chose his words carefully. "I haven't been to church in a long while. My parents took me every Sunday until I left for college. I guess you could say, I haven't really thought about it. Don't get me wrong, I am a believer. I'll go with you. It can't hurt me, but who knows, it may do me some good!"

There were approximately a hundred worshipers in the little church that morning. The brothers agreed that they'd probably shook every hand in the building. "What a friendly bunch of people," Jerry said, "and the sermon was inspiring. I think, I would enjoy this more often."

"I'm glad you enjoyed it," his brother answered, "but I personally found the sermon to be very uncomfortable."

"Uncomfortable? I don't understand, how could it be uncomfortable?"

"I'll tell you about it over breakfast, which I insist on buying. It's about time I start contributing. How about that Bob Evans we passed on the way to church?"

"Sounds good to me. You're buying, so you get to pick the place."

His brother noticed a mood change in Jimmy. He sat moving his food around the plate, without taking a single bite. In an attempt to make conversation, Jerry said, "today was the first time in a long while, I'd been in a church except for weddings and funerals. But, I gotta tell you, the message was exactly what I needed. You told me, you found it uncomfortable. I'm curious, why would that be?"

Jimmy hesitated, pushing his plate aside folding his hands, he looked up at his brother and said, "There's something I need to tell you, something I've never told anyone because I've been so ashamed. The sermon today on forgiveness brought that awful memory back."

"What is it? You can talk to me about anything, that's what brothers are for."

Taking a deep breath and letting it out slowly, Jimmy began, "When I was about nine years old, I was living in a foster home with a middle-aged couple. Their names were John and Sarah Barnes. Sarah was such a nice lady, she read Bible stories to me and taught me the songs we sang in church every Sunday. But John," at this point he teared up trying his best to continue.

"Take your time, Jimmy," Jerry said, reaching over, placing his right hand on his arm.

"One time, late at night, John Barnes came into my room and ah, he did something to me that I'll never forget, something I can't even talk about."

"You don't have to. I know what you're trying to say. This guy was a pedophile, right? He was sick. It wasn't your fault. You have nothing to be ashamed of."

"After that, I kept running away from the house, hiding in the woods. A police officer found me and took me back to Shady Hills Hospital. Today, the pastor spoke on forgiveness, that if you forgive other people when they sin against you, your heavenly father will also forgive you. Every time I read this it eats me up inside. I've tried to forgive him, but I just can't."

They sat in silence while Jerry struggled to reply in an appropriate manner, then remembered what his professor friend used to say, there are times when a listening ear is better than well-meaning advice.

Jimmy took another deep breath while dabbing his eyes with a napkin. "I've kept that buried in my head for years. I feel relieved to finally get it out. Thanks for listening. I'm actually beginning to feel a little better. But, one day, I promise you, I will face John Barnes. I hope when I do, I can say the words, I forgive you.

"We may be twins, but you're a better man than me," Jerry replied. "I don't know if I could do it."

As they walked through the gate of the apartment complex, Jimmy saw a white van with the words, Garden of Eaten Restaurant. This puzzled Jimmy, what would the van be doing here?

The driver side door opened and Chip Francis approached them with his usual five-hundred-watt smile.

"I was just getting ready to leave when I saw you boys. I want to thank you for inviting me to the party, I had a great time last night. But, that's not the reason for my visit this morning."

"What is it? "Jimmy asked.

"Well, I have a birthday present for you. A few years back I had a young kid working part time. A good kid, hard worker, a lot like you, his name was Johnny Miller. He wasn't old enough to get a driver's license, but needed transportation. I loaned him the money to buy a motorized bicycle, which does not require a driver's license.

"To make a long story short, he didn't get along well with his dad's new wife, and things began to go south with his dad as well. He ended up moving to Florida to live with his mother. He insisted on sending me payments for the bike, but I told him to forget about it. Actually, I forgot about that bike until I drove into my garage last night and saw it taking up space. It occurred to me that you could probably make good use of it until you get a driver's license. Come, follow me." Chip opened the back of the van, while gesturing toward a like-new motorbike, and said, "So, what do you think, Jimmy?"

"I think it's exactly what I need. It would take a big strain off my brother, who has been my only transportation. You are not going to believe this. I never, ever, rode even a tricycle before, but it can't be that hard. I'll learn. Also, I'd be happy to pay for it over the next couple months."

"Nonsense, you're doing my wife a favor getting it out of the garage. There is one thing I'd like. When you move up to a car, would you pass the bike on to someone in need? Now I've got to get back to the restaurant," he said, opening the car door. "Don't go out in traffic with that thing until you can handle it. I can't afford to lose a good employee". With that he waved and drove off.

Jerry, being proficient on all kinds of two-wheeled vehicles, took it for a short spin around the parking lot. "This is fun," he said, "the parking lot in the back is deserted. It will be a safe place to practice."

For the rest of the afternoon the brothers rode that little motorbike until it ran out of gas. "Let's go over to the mall," Jerry said. "We'll pick up a gas can, a couple gallons of gas and a bicycle lock. It looks like you've gotten the hang of it, but I suggest you continue walking to work until you feel confident enough to go out in traffic. Tomorrow, I'll stop at the DMV and pick up a Rules of the Road manual. It's one thing to ride well, but it's more important to be safe. By the way, tomorrow I'm going to pay a visit to Lieut. Murphy and get an update on his investigation regarding our mother's assailant."

When Jimmy arrived home from work, the first thing he did was ride his motorbike to the back parking lot and practice several maneuvers until he felt completely at ease. Feeling somewhat proud of himself, he rode back to the carport. While he was busy locking his bike, Jerry drove in.

Stepping out of the car, he waved a small green pamphlet toward his brother. "Got some homework for you Jimmy. It shouldn't take you long to learn how to deal with traffic."

"Thanks, I'll study it tonight. How did things go with Lieut. Murphy?"

"Let's go inside. I'll bring you up-to-date. I can tell you one thing; Lieut. Murphy is a pit bull."

Jimmy took a seat on the couch, while his twin opened the refrigerator and stood taking a visual inventory. "I think I'll have a beer. Would you like anything?"

"A bottle of Pepsi would be good, thanks."

Taking a sip from his beer, Jerry asked, "Have you ever heard of a thing called DNA?"

"No, I can't say that I have," he replied.

"Well, it's a relatively new science that was not available when mom was sexually assaulted. Lieut. Murphy explained that the smallest drop of bodily fluids, or even a single hair, can identify the assailant. It can also identify the parent of a child. Today, Lieut. Murphy swabbed the inside of my mouth with what appeared to be an oversized Q-tip. Tomorrow when he interviews Kyle Phillips, he too will be swabbed. Within a very short time, the forensic scientist can confirm whether or not Kyle is our father. To be honest with you, Jimmy, I shudder to think that we are carrying the genes of that despicable creep."

Jimmy slowly took a sip from his bottle before responding. "Deuteronomy 24:16 tells us, children will not be held accountable for the sins of their father. I don't worry about that. I'm more interested in justice for our mother."

"I never thought about that, but then again, unlike you, I never spent much time reading the good book. Maybe I should start. You know what they say, what doesn't kill you, will make you stronger. At any rate, with a little luck, Lieut. Murphy may have creepy Kyle in handcuffs soon. We'll just have to wait and see."

"Well, if you don't mind," Jimmy said, picking up the pamphlet from the DMV and walking toward his room, "I have a lot of reading to do."

"I glanced over it earlier today, I'm sure you'll find it very helpful."

"I'm sure you're right. I also have to study

what you just referred to as the good book." Then with a wink, he said, "Both are known to save lives. Good night brother, I'll see you in the morning."

The next few days were somewhat uneventful. Jerry received his new assignment from The World Today magazine to write an article on people who've had near death experiences. Jimmy spent his time working, visiting Howard at the park, and becoming very proficient on his motorbike.

One evening after dinner, while they were watching the Cleveland Indians play the Boston Red Sox, the phone rang. Jerry answered on the first ring. It was Lieut. Murphy.

"Hold one second Lieutenant. I want my brother to pick up the extension. We both need to hear this." Holding the phone against his chest, he said, "Jimmy, it's Lieut. Murphy, pick up the extension in my room." After hearing Jimmy say, "I'm here," he continued. "I have my brother on the other line Lieutenant, what do we have?"

"I wish I had better news, but here's what I have so far. When I first met Mr. Phillips, he was very uncooperative and belligerent. He didn't want to talk about anything. He's one tough nut. His attitude changed when I threatened to get a warrant, which would become public information. This spooked him. He not only agreed to this swab test, but also took a polygraph. Long story short, he came up clean. It looks like we're back to square one."

"Square one?" Jimmy blurted, "isn't there something else you can do?"

"Whoa, hold on young man, we're not finished with this case by a long shot. We still have people to interview. As a matter of fact, after looking at that photo again, I discovered there are three other men who work in the general vicinity of Pittsfield. It could be any one of them."

"Who would that be?" Jerry asked.

"There are things I'm not at liberty to discuss on the phone. But, if one or both of you could stop in sometime tomorrow, I can share that information privately."

After hanging up, Jerry waited for his brother to join him. "What do you think? Do you want to join me at the Sheriff's Department tomorrow?"

"Actually, I had plans for tomorrow. I can put them off if you think I should go with you."

"No, I can go alone. I'll take notes. We can

discuss it when I get back. By the way, what are your plans for tomorrow, if you don't mind me asking?"

"I'm going to ride over to Salem. I checked the map, it's only eleven miles from here."

"Salem?" Jerry repeated, "why would you want to go to that sleepy little town?"

"I used to live there," Jimmy said. "I have to deal with something that's been bothering me for years. I need to put it behind me."

"Is it about what happened to you at the foster home?" Jerry asked.

"Yes," he answered. "I made a decision the morning we went to church together. Do you remember what the pastor said about forgiveness?"

"He said a lot of things. I was very impressed with his sermon. I would like to go back again. What did he say that convinced you to visit that evil bastard?"

"The pastor said, sometimes, it's better to bury the past than to bear it. Tomorrow, I'm going to do just that."

"I'm sure you know what you're doing. Just be careful that your emotions don't take over and things get out of hand." Putting both hands onto Jimmy's shoulders he said, "I just got my brother out of one terrible place. I don't need to be bailing him out of jail."

"Don't worry, that's not going to happen. It is written," he said, pausing to be sure he quoted the Scripture correctly, "if anyone slaps you on the right cheek, turn to them the other cheek also."

"Wow, I have a college degree, but I swear I've gotten more wisdom from you in three months than I did in four years of college. Keep it up. You'll have me reading that book. You really have it together, Jimmy. Be careful on the road. We'll talk tonight. Hopefully we'll both have a successful day."

CHAPTER SIXTEEN

It was a pleasant ride to Salem that morning, very little traffic. The weather was perfect. Riding past the First Baptist Church of Salem brought memories flooding back. The songs, bible stories and a game called bible trivia. Answer the question correctly, you get a prize, everything from candy to a children's Christian book. Mrs. Barnes made sure everybody got something. Those were happy times until that night his world was shattered.

Walking up to the door of that house on Elm Street, Jimmy whispered a silent prayer for God's guidance. The house was a different color now, but everything else was familiar. He wiped the sweat from his hands, rubbing them on his pants, before ringing the doorbell. Hearing footsteps approaching. He took a deep breath. The door opened and there stood Mrs. Barnes, slightly older, still resembling a character out of Little House on the Prairie.

"Can I help you, young man?" she said. Her voice, along with her warm smile, was the same as he remembered.

"Hello Mrs. Barnes," Jimmy said, smiling down at her. "Do you remember me?"

"You certainly do look familiar," she said shading her eyes with her hand. Squinting up at him, "Were you one of the kids in my Sunday school class?"

"I was. I lived in this house for a while. My name is Jimmy Simmons."

"Oh! my Lord," she screamed. "Oh, my Lord." Her eyes filled with tears as she began to shake uncontrollably. "I've been praying for you since the day you left," she said in a whisper.

He hugged her as she sobbed, clinging to him.

"Come in, come in, Lord have mercy, I was afraid I'd never see you again."

He followed her into the kitchen. It felt to him like a time warp, as though he had been there only yesterday.

"Sit down Jimmy, please. I'll make some tea. Or would you like coffee, milk, water?" she rambled nervously, wringing her hands. "Please forgive me, but seeing you again is such a shock."

"A cup of tea would be nice," he said. "I just want to sit and visit with you for a while, it's been a long time."

"I made oatmeal cookies last night. Do you remember my oatmeal cookies?"

"I do. You made the best oatmeal cookies I've ever had," he said, smiling.

They sat in silence for a while just looking at each other.

"Jimmy, you are a sight for sore eyes," she gushed. "Tell me, what have you been up to? Where do you live? What kind of work do you do?"

"It's been tough at times, Mrs. Barnes. I was shuffled from one foster home to another, one institution to another. Lately though, I have been blessed. I found my only brother after twenty-five years. We're twins, you know. I live about ten miles from here. I have a decent job. But never mind me, it's such a blessing to see you after all this time."

Wanting to steer the conversation away from himself, he summoned the courage to ask, "Where is Mr. John?"

While fidgeting with the small gold cross on a chain she wore around her neck, she looked directly into Jimmy's eyes. Showing no emotion, she said, "Mr. John is dead."

"Dead?" Jimmy said after a stretch of silence, "Mrs. Barnes, I'm so sorry."

"Shh," she whispered, placing her index finger over her lips. "I'm not sorry. You shouldn't be either. I think I know what happened to you Jimmy, why you were so afraid of him. Shortly after we were dropped from the foster care program, John volunteered to work with the youth group at church. One day, while on a mission trip, he molested a young boy. That little boy ran away, just like you used to do. When the police found him, he told them what John did to him. John was arrested. Our name was all over the newspapers. It was so humiliating. During his trial, three more boys came forward with the same story. Jimmy, I can't tell you how sorry I am."

Reaching across the table, gently holding both her hands, Jimmy replied, "You don't have anything to be sorry for. It wasn't your fault."

"But I was your foster mother. I dreamed of adopting you. Dreamed of being your forever mother. Mothers are supposed to protect their children. I failed you. Every single day, I've prayed for you and the other three boys. Do you remember how John couldn't complete a sentence without quoting scriptures from the Bible?"

"Yes, I remember," Jimmy answered softly.

"I don't understand it, Jimmy, how could someone constantly quote God's word, yet do such an evil thing to innocent children?"

"That isn't for us to judge. The scripture says, *I will take revenge; I will pay them back, says the Lord.*"

"I know. I know. I don't have the right to judge people. It's so hard not to. I wish I was stronger. You know, Jimmy, when the prison chaplain called to tell me John was dead, I didn't shed a tear. But I've shed a million tears for you and the other children."

For the next few moments neither of them spoke a word.

Jimmy broke the silence asking her, "How did Mr. John die?"

"He was killed by three inmates in prison. It seems even the most despicable criminals despise child molesters. One night three men who had been sentenced to life, with nothing more to lose, beat John to death." Overcome with emotion, she hesitated saying anything more, attempting to gain her composure. Rising, she pushed back from the table. "I'm so sorry to be going on like this, but until you showed up today, I've been keeping everything bottled up inside. Jimmy, let me get us some more tea."

He watched while Mrs. Barnes poured their tea. He wanted to console her, but sensed there was more she needed to say.

She continued. "I stay home alone mostly, except for grocery shopping and church. I can only imagine what people are thinking. I used to be so close with my neighbor, Grace, but since the trial, she has been avoiding me."

"Mrs. Barnes, she's probably uncomfortable and doesn't know what to say, or how to say it. Have you reached out to her at all?"

"No, I haven't, now that you mention it."

"I bet if you paid her a visit, everything would soon be back to normal. Maybe even take her some of these world-class cookies," he said with a smile while reaching for another one. "You may have to be the one to break the ice."

"I must admit, I've spent a lot of time fretting and feeling sorry for myself. I just feel like I should have known what was going on."

"Let me tell you something, if not for you, I probably wouldn't be a believer today. Remember those Bible stories you told me as a child? Remember the songs we sang?"

A slight smile appeared on her lips as she nodded, "Yes, yes I do."

At that point, Jimmy began to sing softly. "This little light of mine, I'm gonna let it shine. This little light of mine, I'm gonna let it shine."

Mrs. Barnes smiled brightly, swaying to the song, conducting with her hands as she began to sing along. She clapped her hands together saying, "Remember this one?" Drumming her fingers on the table, "Jesus loves the little children, all the children of the world." As Jimmy joined in, the joy on her face soared to new heights.

Glancing at his watch, Jimmy exclaimed, "Oh my gosh, I promised my brother I'd be home by four. I'm going to have to go now, Mrs. Barnes, but I promise I'll come back and see you again."

Walking toward the door, she stopped.

"What is it?" Jimmy asked.

"I want you to know, this has been the best day I've had in a long time. You will come back again soon? Be sure to call ahead, so I can bake your favorite cookies."

She stood on the front porch waving, until Jimmy was completely out of sight.

CHAPTER SEVENTEEN

"Well, there is my little brother," Jerry said, as Jimmy entered the apartment. "I see you're still in one piece. How'd the confrontation go?" he asked sliding his papers aside, laying his pencil down.

"Younger brother, not little brother! I'm almost an inch taller and one-half shoe size larger!" Jimmy quipped. "There was no confrontation, John Barnes was murdered in prison, leaving poor Mrs. Barnes a basket case. I wasn't the only person he assaulted. Three other boys in his church were victims. Mrs. Barnes somehow blames herself for what happened. I think she needed someone to listen because, by the time I left, we were singing, laughing and reminiscing about Sunday school. I believe she's going to be okay now. I promised to visit her again, to keep in touch. How'd your day go?"

"When I got to the Sheriff's office this morning, he'd left a message with the receptionist saying he'd call me later. Something urgent had just come up. I haven't heard from him so far. With nothing else to do, I drove over to Steve Abrams office."

"Steve Abrams, isn't he the attorney that set up my release from Bainbridge?"

"Yep, he's the one. I was filling out the legal forms he gave me when you walked in. Our plan is to get Mom released from Pittsfield as soon as possible. I spoke to my mother in Colorado today. She offered to research suitable nursing homes in the area. I was so proud she would do that. I asked her if she was offended by all the attention I've been giving my birth mother. You wanna hear what she said, Jimmy?"

"What did she say?"

"She said, 'Jerry, you have enough love for two mothers. I want you to tell Jimmy, that I have enough love for two sons.'"

"Wow, that's so sweet, she must be a wonderful person."

"Anyway, Steve Abrams tells me that Mom's

case will be much simpler than yours."

"So, if everything goes as planned, we could be headed to Colorado in a couple weeks, three at the most. If you promised Mrs. Barnes a visit, you may want to do it sooner rather than later. I did some checking, but before making a decision, I wanted to run it past you. I'm afraid flying by air could be traumatic for Mom. So, I checked with Amtrak. Their sleeper car rates are less than airline tickets. It's thirty-eight hours from Cleveland to Colorado Springs, with some beautiful sights to see along the way. Don't you think that would be more relaxing?"

"Since I've never been on a train or plane, I'll leave that decision up to you. It would be good to have a female to help Mom with whatever women need."

"I've got that covered too. I called Anna Frances and asked if she knew of anybody we could hire to take care of that. She said, 'As a matter of fact, I do. I have a lot of vacation and personal time stored up. I've never been to Colorado, and always dreamed of traveling cross-country by train. So, I'm your girl, if you want me.'"

"You're amazing, big brother. I can't believe you accomplished all that in one day. I'll be sure to give notice to Chip at the restaurant, visit with Howard at the park and visit Mrs. Barnes one more time."

"I'll drink to that," Jerry said. As he walked toward the refrigerator to get a beer, the phone rang.

He answered on the first ring.

"Jerry, this is Lieut. Murphy. I don't have time to talk right now but I want you and your brother to watch the 6 o'clock news. That's about five minutes from now, don't miss it." Jerry hurried to the TV, turning to channel 5.

"Breaking news," they heard the reporter announce. "The twenty-five-year-old rape case at Pittsfield Psychiatric Hospital was solved today. Our cameras were on location in the affluent community of Shaker Heights filming the arrest."

Both brothers bolted from their seats, their eyes glued to the T.V. as they witnessed two deputies leading a man in handcuffs. As they came closer, Jimmy's jaw dropped as he whispered, "Oh my God, it can't be, that can't be him."

"It's him," Jerry exclaimed, "it's him, no mistake about it. It's Graves."

The reporter went on to say,"This story came

from a series of coincidences that prompted Lieut. Ryan Murphy of Summit County Sheriff's Department to reopen the case that went cold in 1965. A young Colorado Springs journalist whose pen name is Kevin Langford unwittingly discovered documents in his parent's attic showing that he was adopted from an agency called Kinder Kare in Summit County. Mr. Langford came to Northeastern Ohio in search of his birth parents, only to find his mother was a patient at Pittsfield Psychiatric Hospital. She was also the victim of a heinous rape. After a tenacious investigation, Mr. Langford, whose birth name was Gerald Simmons, discovered he has a fraternal twin. We'll have more on this story when additional information comes available. We'll be right back."

During the commercial, the brothers sat quietly, at a loss for words. When the phone rang, Jerry motioned for his brother to pick up the extension phone.

"This is Lieut. Murphy. Did you catch it?"

"We did, we're still in a state of shock. How did you nail that perverted scum bag?"

"First, we did a little experiment at the hospital with your mother. One of our female detectives, Liz Richards visited with her. Throughout the visit she showed Rachel several random pictures. Whenever she saw a picture of Dr. Graves, she became somewhat agitated. Then, she showed her a picture of Graves from twenty years ago. This time, Rachel went absolutely ballistic, she tore the picture to shreds and began pulling her hair. Liz said she'd never seen anything like it. Based on that, we brought Graves in for questioning. He was very uncooperative, refusing a polygraph or a saliva swab. He went through a bunch of dramatic motions, waving a very expensive Meerschaum pipe, pointing it at us. Then, like some movie star, he would lean back and hold that pipe in his mouth with the most superior look on his face. We didn't have enough evidence to hold him, so we let him go. He stood looking down at us with a very indignant expression and stormed out the door. The brilliant Rhodes Scholar made one mistake. Unfortunately for him, he left his pipe behind. His DNA matched yours, so with probable cause, we had the legal right to forcibly collect his DNA. Again, it was a perfect match. Dr. Graves is proven to be your biological father."

"I would never use the word father to describe that creep," Jerry said. "He's nothing more than a perverted sexual predator. I hope he rots in hell. What do you think, Jimmy?"

"I won't waste my time thinking about him. He'll get what's coming to him. I'm just glad this is over, so we can concentrate on doing what's best for our mother."

Lieut. Murphy broke in. "I'm gonna sign off now. If you boys need anything, you know where to find me."

Jimmy walked slowly back into the living room shaking his head.

Jerry was the first to speak. "I have such mixed emotions right now. I'm happy to have the case solved. I am relieved that the creep will be off the streets. But, what troubles me is our family gene pool. The thought of his blood running through my veins is enough to make me puke."

"I see things differently regarding our gene pool," Jimmy replied as he sat across from his brother and, leaning forward with an earnest expression, began. "We inherit things like height, eye color, and intelligence. We don't in-herit evil desires. If one person in a family is an ax murderer, that has nothing to do with their genes. Our morals, yours and mine, are based solely on decisions we make. Yes, Graves is our biological father, who chose to do a terrible thing. He is also a Rhodes Scholar. Our mother was a brilliant Phi Beta Kappa, who graduated summa cum laude. I feel blessed that we've inherited those genes. So, our destiny – as I see it – is inherited due to our choices."

"I love your positive attitude, kid."

"Thanks, old man," Jimmy answered.

"Seriously, your attitude is amazing, especially considering what you've been through."

"Thanks Jerry, but I don't have to look far to find someone who's been through worse. *It is written, in this world you will have trouble, but take heart, for I have overcome the world.*"

"I swear," Jerry said chuckling, "you're going to have me reading that book one day."

"You should try it, it's a great read. It's been on the bestseller list for hundreds of years!"

"You may be right Jimmy, but right now we have some planning to do. It looks like our work here is almost finished."

* * *

Eleven days later, four people boarded a train. One on vacation, one going home and two in search of a new life. *We have to celebrate and be glad, because this brother of yours was dead and is alive again. He was lost and is found.*

EPILOGUE

Armed with solid DNA evidence, the state prosecutor had an ironclad case against Dr. Graves. It took the jury one hour thirty minutes to find the defendant guilty of aggravated rape. He was sentenced to fifteen years in the Ohio State Penitentiary, the same facility that housed the notorious mobster, Bugsy Malone, as well as the infamous Dr. Sam Shepard. Ironically, poetic justice caught up with the narcissistic aristocrat. This egotistic Rhodes Scholar will spend the next fifteen years mopping floors and scrubbing toilets. Unlike his days as director of several state psychiatric institutions, he will not enjoy the same esteem from his new neighbors.

Anna Frances spent two weeks enjoying the beautiful area in and around Colorado Springs. Reluctant to leave the scenic mountains, she promised to return again. She boarded a plane to Cleveland, looking forward to returning home to her friends and colleagues. Shortly after arriving home, she was pleasantly surprised to receive a phone call from the Governor. He offered her the position of Regional Director; the same position once held by Dr. Herbert Graves. Anna accepted. She immediately put policy changes in place to improve the quality of care for the patients. She had broached the subject many times with Dr. Graves, who dismissed it as unnecessary. She received personal visits, phone calls, and letters from practically every employee, expressing their congratulations and best wishes.

Rachel is living in a beautiful upscale assisted living facility called Mountain View Home in Colorado Springs. With the extra attention and intense therapy, she is making excellent progress. She is now able to verbalize short sentences, such as, thank you, coffee please, and I love you. When the twins walk into her room, she reaches out smiling and says, "My boys."

Two years later ... The brothers co-wrote an autobiography under their birth names, Gerald and James Simmons. The heartwarming story was immediately picked up by the national media. They were guests on Good Morning America, The Tonight Show, and Opera Winfrey. With extensive media publicity, the book made the New York Times bestseller list for seven months. Gerald went on to be a popular author, writing novels and short stories under his pen name Kevin Lankford.

Jimmy methodically implemented his plans. First a driver's license, followed by a Graduate Equivalent Degree. He enrolled at Nazarene Bible College in Colorado Springs, earning a Degree in Biblical Studies. As an Ordained Minister, he took a job as the Youth Pastor at Living Waters Community Church. Due to the popularity of his book, he became a highly sought-after inspirational speaker. He was also a popular guest speaker at churches around the country.

On one such occasion, while speaking at a church in Northeastern Ohio, he went by the park to visit his old friend Howard, only to learn he passed away six months earlier. Before leaving town, he paid a short visit to Mrs. Barnes. He learned that everything was back to normal for her with her friends and neighbors. She didn't hesitate to thank Jimmy and let him know the importance of his last visit. After a cup of tea, along with two delicious oatmeal cookies, he left, promising to keep in touch by phone.

When time permits, Jimmy volunteers at homeless shelters, jails and prisons. He was thrilled to officiate the wedding of his brother, along with friends, family and most importantly, his mother sitting proudly in the front row. During the ceremony he was overjoyed to see the smiling face of Dale Karsten sitting near the back with his wife and three children. He'd heard Dale finally got the little girl they had been praying for.

During the reception, he spent a great deal of time reminiscing with Dale. He re-lived his days at Shady Hills, how Dale taught him to swim, and the Thanksgiving Day he'd never forget. How he could still smell the aroma of that delicious Thanksgiving dinner. Jimmy spoke of everything as though it happened yesterday. From the nature trail at Raintree State Park where he walked the suspension bridge over the river, the petting zoo, and his first hot fudge sundae. He explained how devastated he was on that day returning to Shady Hills. His saddest memory, however, was the day he learned that Dale had moved to Pennsylvania.

The best memory, however, was the day Dale and his brother Gerald visited him at Pittsfield with the joyous news that soon he would at last be free. Those memories would last forever. After the reception, their conversation went well into the night. The next morning, Jimmy drove the Karsten family to the airport, but not before planning a visit in the near future.

Jimmy's days were spent with family, countless friends, and exploring all of what he had missed over the years. He became enamored with a petite brunette named Melissa Owens, an elementary school teacher, and worship leader at Living Waters Community Church. Six months later, they were engaged. They set a wedding date for the following June.

Jimmy anxiously awaits that special day when his dreams of having his own family are fulfilled. He often falls asleep thinking, what a storybook life. What a destiny I inherited.

About the Authors

Dan's career spanned many years in Sales and Marketing, primarily in the seafood industry. Dan served as Vice President of Sales and Marketing with several national and international firms, while Susan worked as a purchasing agent for an international tuna importer and served as President of a food brokerage company.

After retiring, Dan attended Moody Bible Institute and became an ordained minister, serving incarcerated inmates.

Dan's love of writing began when he was a young man and culminated with the debut and publication of his first thriller novel, The Cost of Living, in the Spring of 2019.

Dan and Susan continue to work with a local homeless mission and find relaxation collaborating on this second novel, Inherited Destiny, from their home in Clearwater, Florida.